CHOCOLATE CHERRY CABIN

A SECOND CHANCE SINGLE MOM CHRISTMAS ROMANCE

HOCKEY SWEETHEARTS
BOOK THREE

JEAN ORAM

Chocolate Cherry Cabin
A Second Chance Single Mom Christmas Romance

A Hockey Sweethearts Novel
By Jean Oram

First Large Print Edition 2022

Cover design by Jean Oram

Complete cataloguing information available online or upon request.

Oram, Jean.

Chocolate Cherry Cabin: A Second Chance Single Mom Christmas Romance / Jean Oram.—1st. ed.

ISBN: 978-1-990833-30-4 (paperback), 978-1-990833-29-8 (large print), 978-1-990833-28-1 9ebook)

First Oram Productions Large Print Edition: November 2022

1

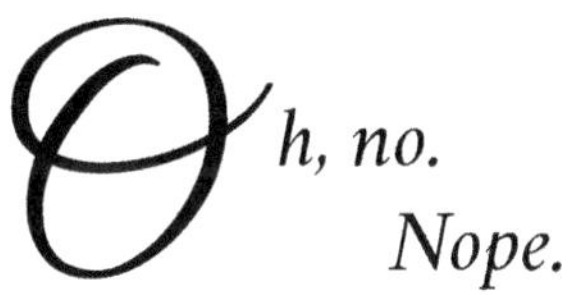*h, no.*

Nope.

There was no way Louis Bellmore was her new neighbor.

Hannah was going to toss that thought straight from her mind and keep hanging her outdoor Christmas lights and ignore the tall figure in the yard behind her. She adored the month of December, and thinking about that man would ruin her mood with fabulous efficiency.

Think about Christmas. Think about the way the holidays bring people together, highlighting their innate kindness and generosity.

Unlike Louis, who had been horrible to her in

high school. Always judging, always acting as though her plan to marry her high school sweetheart wasn't enough.

Hannah yanked at her lights. They were too loose. How had Calvin always made them look so perfect?

As she struggled with the tangle of wires she caught a glimpse of her seven-year-old tearing by with his elbow out—a sure sign he was attempting another wrestling move on the inflatable snowman in the front yard.

"Thomas, cut it out! You're going to wreck poor Frosty."

"He had it coming! He's a wily, frozen-headed monster!'"

Hannah readjusted the ladder, shifting it around the corner, then did a double-take as she peeked back at Thomas, who was now running in the opposite direction.

"Tom-Tom, you better not have done that!"

There was a telling silence and Hannah groaned. She was fairly certain he'd just stuck his tongue out at Mrs. Fisher, the Longhorn Diner's waitress. She was a good woman, but very efficient in spreading gossip. The last thing Hannah needed was word getting out that, as a day care worker, she couldn't keep her own kids under control.

"What have I said about being polite?" Hannah called into the yard.

"Okay. I will."

"Apologize. Right now."

"She didn't see me."

"Do it anyway."

"Sorry, Mrs. Fisher!" he yelled.

Hannah waited to hear the woman reply, then climbed the ladder. Where had Thomas learned his wrestling moves? Surely not from his father, who was mild-mannered and on the same parenting page as she was. Other single moms might worry about the impact of their ex's lax rules and schedules, but Thomas was given the same boundaries when he was at Calvin's house, which meant no wrestling. No sticking out of tongues, either.

Maybe Thomas was picking up things from his older brother Wade? Ever since the separation a year and a half ago, and then the subsequent divorce, Wade had been more physical in expressing himself.

From the ladder, Hannah could see that Thomas had managed to wrangle the seven-foot-tall snowman into a headlock. Their golden retriever, a rescued dog that Thomas had renamed Obi-Wan Kenobi after the *Star Wars* character, was barking and dancing as though a stranger had entered the yard.

"What was I thinking, buying that snowman?" she muttered. Wade had been in love with the idea of snow, and he'd requested the yard decoration as well as mitts so he could pretend he lived in Alaska instead of sunny Texas. She'd quickly got on board, hoping to coax more smiles from her eldest. Instead he'd rejected it all once Thomas got excited about it.

"Obi, hush!" Hannah called. "And Thomas, cut it out. You're getting the dog excited!"

Something caught her eye as the canine continued to bark. There *was* a stranger, although not in their yard. The new neighbor, who'd moved in a few weeks ago, was rolling some fancy grill, which had likely cost as much as all the furniture in her living room, from his truck. She watched him go behind the fence and hedge that separated the two yards, and around to the back of his house.

This man had the same lanky build and improbably wide shoulders, but it couldn't be Louis. There was no way he'd move back home to Sweetheart Creek. Like she and Calvin, and so many of their classmates, he'd left town after high school. In fact, the last time she'd seen Louis he'd been across the street from the police station, smirking, as she'd shuffled out with her parents, shoulders hunched and completely mortified.

One day she might think the graduation prank had been funny. Her friends April and Jackie already did, but that was likely because they'd been the ones to dare her to join them and hadn't been caught. Their horses had been faster, their riding skills impressive. In their identity-masking costumes they'd ridden through the school hallways, vanishing almost as fast as they'd appeared.

Hannah less so. Once inside, her horse had balked, and she'd been so afraid of hitting her head on a door jamb that she'd been busted almost immediately.

That would have been okay, but one of the teachers had spooked her horse, which promptly kicked in the football trophy case, then left behind a stinky, steaming pile.

One of the many cowboy students had settled the horse and led it back outside with her astride, inadvertently delivering her to the waiting sheriff.

She'd earned a bit of street cred for performing the dare, and would have felt proud if Louis hadn't been there, waiting and smirking outside the police station when her parents had sprung her loose.

If it really was him next door, it would only figure that he'd return to town now, when she was working on cleaning up the implosion of her meticulously planned life. The plans he'd scoffed at.

It had over a decade, but just thinking about Louis still had the power to rile her.

It couldn't be him next door, though. Sure, her neighbor had that same tightly-packed brawn, but Louis was coaching for the NHL now. He wouldn't choose to live in a small house beside her old cabin. He had the means to buy something nicer. Much nicer.

Plus he was a man of adventure, and Sweetheart Creek was so quiet. There wasn't much more than barn dances and a cranky armadillo that chased people down Main Street when it came to entertainment.

And since it couldn't be Louis, she needed to shove aside her introverted nature and bring him a plate of her semi-famous chocolate cherry cookies. Not the burned ones, or the ones where

Thomas had gone nuts with the chocolate chips, but the nice ones.

The neighbor came back through his side yard, causing Obi to bark again. His jacket was zipped up to his chin, and Hannah couldn't quite make out his features even from her perch on the ladder. But when the dog let out another bark, the man turned, and Hannah caught a very familiar blue-eyed gaze. She let out a yelp as her foot slipped on the rung, nearly sending her tumbling to the ground.

It *was* Louis. Louis Bellmore.

No, no, no, no. No! What had she done to deserve him as her neighbor? She was a good person. Karma should be on her side, not working against her!

She didn't dare look back his way, but with her head spinning, carefully climbed down to the safety of the dry earth. It was simply her imagination playing games with her. There was no reason for Louis to return to this small, quiet town when he was all about flash and adventure. Sure, his dad still lived here, but he could visit between coaching games for the San Antonio Dragons, based a little more than an hour away.

Maybe he'd bought the house to rent it out, or flip it.

Yes, that must be what he was doing. It would all be okay.

He was just spending a lot of time here working on it and moving stuff into it because…

Hannah sighed, unable to deny the truth any longer.

Louis Bellmore, her former nemesis, was her neighbor, and nearly falling off the ladder had likely given him something to laugh about.

Louis smiled and began heading toward Hannah Murphy's yard. Finally a chance to meet. He'd seen her peeking through the crack in her curtains when the moving truck arrived with his stuff a few weeks ago. She'd done a good job of avoiding bumping into him, always in a rush to or from her car.

Truthfully, he'd been avoiding her, too. Sure, he was busy coaching and trying to resuscitate a poorly ranked hockey team, and could use that as an excuse. It was more than that, though. If he didn't see her, he could pretend she'd gotten over whatever it was that had set her off all those years ago. He could imagine a chance to make a new first impression with her and even picture them becoming friends.

He came around the edge of the white fence that separated the two properties, counting his blessings with his job, his new house in the town he considered home, being closer to his dad, who lived only a few blocks away—and Hannah.

Be polite. Be nice, he reminded himself. *Don't share your thoughts on her life unless nagged to. And even then, try to avoid opening your mouth.*

His straight-down-the-pipe opinions worked in the national hockey league, but they weren't as well received by women—and especially Hannah.

Her dog was barking, but stayed at a distance as Louis approached Hannah and her ladder. Then, as if it couldn't help itself, it started wagging its tail and came closer.

"Hannah Murphy?" Louis said.

He could tell she'd heard him by the way her body stiffened, but she acted like she was too focused on untangling her lights to have heard him. He sighed inwardly. She still held a grudge. It looked as though this was where his good luck, second chances, karma and all that good energy that had brought him home again ran out.

He stopped beside her.

"Hey, Louis. How's it going?" she said casually

—too casually. She glanced over at his house and swallowed hard.

"Uh, good. And you?"

"Good," she said evenly. "Really good."

He had a feeling she'd lie through her teeth about how good things were due to how hard he'd been on her during high school. But what had he expected? She'd had every bone in the human body memorized long before he'd ever met her in the tenth grade. Then she'd given it all up for that doofus Calvin Kendrick. Louis had noticed the guy zip up in a fancy car the other night, then take off with two young boys. Her sons, he guessed, and Calvin the father. But were they divorced? It looked that way. Plus, she hadn't corrected him when he'd called her by her maiden name. And she definitely would have corrected him if she was still married.

"Are you...?" Hannah gestured vaguely in the direction of Louis's new place.

"Am I your neighbor? Yeah." He crossed his arms, watching her reaction, realizing he was echoing her body language. The familiar old standoff. Defensive mechanisms engaged.

Louis sighed. He'd stupidly thought this would be so much easier, due to the passing of time. Just walk in, smile, show her he wasn't actually that bad of a human being, and convince her to be friends.

Then at some point she'd realize he was actually kind of handsome and nice to have around, and within a few years—or months—they'd be married.

In reality, he seemed to still be firmly inked in on her enemies list.

"Well then, welcome to the neighborhood," she said with that Texas drawl that tickled his insides. It left him feeling warm even when she was miffed at him.

She gave what might have passed as a friendly smile among T. rexes, and turned to deal with her dangling lights.

Her dog, who had been creeping closer and closer, was finally leaning against Louis's shin, and he bent to give him a vigorous ear rub. The animal grinned up at him, pink tongue lolling to the side, but then its ears perked up and it zipped off around the corner of the house.

Louis figured he should probably go. Hannah's welcome was about as awesome-feeling as the moment she'd pulled his name out of Mr. Chen's hat in biology class and locked herself in as his secret Santa. He'd known she had his name the moment she'd sagged in her seat, eyes closing.

She'd got him something good, though. Thoughtful. A pocket knife even nicer than the cheap T-shirt she'd bought for Calvin, her boyfriend. Louis had never been able to acknowledge the gift, though. She hadn't fessed up to it, and he'd pretended he thought it was from one of his admirers.

Not wanting to head back to his house and cement in this awkward moment as the basis for their future relationship, as Hannah climbed the ladder, Louis fed her the string of lights so she could attach them to the eaves.

"How long have you been back in town?" he asked, wincing at her handiwork. The strand hung unevenly, and she hadn't put the ladder in the right spot. She was having to reach farther out than was safe. He untangled a few knots while she worked above, doing his best to brace the wobbling ladder at the same time.

"A year," she muttered.

"How's Sweetheart Creek? Has it changed much? I noticed there's an armadillo on the welcome sign now."

"Yeah," she said, after a moment of silence. "That's Bill. Best to avoid him."

Kind of like his hockey team's PR squad,

headed by Nuvella. Best to avoid her when possible.

“Other than that,” Hannah was saying, “it’s the same. Changed, but the same.”

“Kind of sums up life, right?” Louis said, squinting up at her.

He’d lived in the small town only a few years, but it had felt more like home than where he’d grown up in Colorado. He’d left hockey behind when he’d moved here as a teen, but the game had now brought him back, like the completion of a circle.

He’d been bitter moving away from the life he’d known, away from hockey, but attention from the local girls had been a salve to his teen ego. Moving to town as an athletic sixteen-year-old had been like walking into a tiger’s den, as fresh meat.

Louis had thought he would play the field, but then he’d met Hannah. Smart, quiet, kind. With big dreams for medical school. The longer she’d dated Calvin, the more that dream had seemed to fade, until all she talked about was marriage.

Louis hated that he’d called her complaisant. That he’d made it crystal clear to her that he believed she did things to please others and not herself. He’d hated it even more that she’d known the difference between complacent and complaisant, and that she'd known exactly what he'd been calling her in that moment. The word had hit her like an insult, taking her down a peg.

It still made him itch with discomfort.

But Calvin? Come on. She could have done so much better.

One thing that hadn't changed about Louis was his looks. He was still handsome. More mature and manly, of course, but still good-looking enough to set her heart aflutter. She'd felt it the first time she'd met him, despite having just started dating Calvin. Because, really? Whose wouldn't flutter? Louis was tall, hunky and smart. He had some Blackfoot or Ojibwe roots that had gifted him with glorious black hair and a strong nose that most men would be proud to have grace their silhouette.

The girls in her class had gone nuts over him. He'd been new and different, with adventures from the outside world. Louis would mysteriously vanish at lunchtime, never saying where he'd gone, just giving this slightly haunted half smile when anyone asked. He was instantly cool.

Initially, Hannah had thought he was a nice guy, but the moment he'd seen Calvin slide his arm possessively around her shoulders, he'd turned opinionated. He hadn't seen that she was secure about her life and dreams, but had accused her of doing everything to please others.

What would a guy like him know, anyway? He thrived on chaos and on frustrating people, which was so completely *not* what she was about. Anger burned through Hannah, igniting old memories and wounds.

With Louis feeding her the lights it had taken mere moments to attach the next length to the eaves. Having reached out as far as she could, she had to scamper down to shift the ladder.

As soon as her feet touched the ground, Louis was there, nudging her aside. "Let me," he murmured, then moved the ladder over several feet.

"I can do it," she argued, her attempts to elbow him out of the way failing. He had climbed up in a flash and was already reaching along the eaves, attaching the lights, his jacket rising above his belt, revealing what appeared to be a bronzed midriff.

"Why are you tanned?" she blurted. "It's December."

"Doesn't make me popular, but it's something

I do every year." Seeing her confused look, he added, "Morocco. I go over there to do volunteer work."

"Without your shirt on?"

He chuckled. "There are beaches. Plus it gets pretty hot."

Why was her breath sticking in her lungs? He wasn't her type. She needed a man who was content to curl up and watch movies through the winter nights, not go spend time helping people.

Obviously, her priorities were way off when it came to men, because his life sounded kind of fabulous.

Too bad he was such a judgmental jerk.

Not that they'd ever date. He would never be the type a single mom could count on. Plus there was the whole thing where the first one to fall asleep would be murdered by the other. Hannah had loathed being his partner in chemistry, even though it had been outright freeing how she could banter and make digs at him, no holds barred. She could insult him and he'd grin, somehow loving her moxie. How he'd never taken it personally was a skill she'd love to learn.

"What have you been up to?" he asked, as he angled himself to climb down.

Not anything as cool as volunteering in foreign countries.

"I can do the lights," she said politely, steadying the ladder as he descended.

"You still with Calvin?" he asked, his gaze fixed on the eaves above.

Hannah sighed loudly and climbed the ladder as soon as he'd moved it. "Why? Are you looking to butt heads with him for old times' sake?" She glared down at Louis, hating the way he'd made her doubt her decisions as a teen. Hating the way he'd been right to do so.

He smirked, a familiar expression that would surely grow when he learned that her marriage—just as he'd predicted—hadn't lasted.

Sweetheart Creek was small, and she knew he'd have the answer soon enough if he didn't already. He was probably asking only so he could deliver an I-told-you-so.

"I'm not," Hannah admitted, coming down to move the ladder once again. Why did it still hurt to admit that her marriage had failed?

Louis's calculating blue eyes met hers, and she lashed out before he could say anything, asking, "And are you still with any girl who'll smile at you?"

The way his lips danced with amusement

while he looked at her in that direct way of his stole her breath. There was something about him that challenged her, made her feel alive, unhinged and...irritated. Very, very irritated.

Having him next door was not going to be good for the inner peace she had been trying to cultivate since Calvin had informed her he didn't actually love her any longer.

She started to shift the ladder, but Louis was holding it in place, still watching her with amusement.

"How's that fast lifestyle working for you?" She jerked it from his grip. "Got anyone pregnant?"

"No, not yet. How's your quiet life?"

"I *like* my life." She snatched the string of lights and stormed up the rungs.

"I'm sure you do," he replied mildly. "Dr. Murphy?"

His tone was innocent, but something inside Hannah snapped. He'd been there when her dream of becoming a doctor had cruised right into a brick wall—or rather, flopped into his arms in a dead faint. He knew darn well why she hadn't gone to medical school. Her friends had simply shrugged when she'd told them of her change of plans. But Louis? He'd made it all about Calvin, like her boyfriend had something to do with the fact that she fainted at the sight of blood.

"I have the important things, and it's *rewarding*." A plastic clip for the lights broke, and went flying into the dry grass below. Wordlessly, Louis reached into the sack of extra clips hanging off the ladder and handed her a new one.

"So is volunteering. You should try it."

"It's called my current job," she muttered, thinking of how Tonya had managed to snag more hours at Colts and Fillies than she had over the holiday season. The day care would be closed for a few days over Christmas, the hours already reduced as more parents took time off work, but not getting even half her share of hours had hurt.

"You volunteer? Where?"

"I was kidding. But I do volunteer at the boys' school when—"

"Mom!"

The panic in Thomas's voice made Hannah clutch the ladder and snap her head in his direction. "What's wrong?"

He was holding his pale blue mittens under his bleeding nose. His gushing nose.

Lots of blood. And oh so red…

Her head grew light, just as it had in biology class when she was seventeen. Hannah clung to the ladder, trying to steady herself as she stumbled down the rungs.

"You're okay, Thomas," she said, trying to soothe him as her vision began to narrow, like headlights dimming on a dark winter's night as the car battery began to die.

Not here. Not now. Not in front of Louis. And definitely not in front of Thomas.

"I've got you," Louis said, and she let out a breath of relief. At least someone could help her boy.

Hannah jolted when Louis's large hands landed on her waist to help her descend. Once she was on the ground, he gently directed her to perch on the bottom wrung of the ladder, her head between her knees. She almost wished she'd pass out so she could skip over this humiliating moment.

"You're okay," he said calmly. His firm hand on her back was soothing, and her vision slowly returned.

Obi was barking, jumping around them.

"It's okay, doggy. Yeah, just helping Hannah," Louis said, his voice deep and calming. Man, she hated that beautiful voice. Obi-Wan pranced about, his tail whacking her in the leg, his nose nudging her.

"It's okay, Obi," she said. "You're okay, too, Thomas," she called. "Just keep holding your mitten to your nose. It'll stop soon. And go inside. Wade will help you, and I'll come in, too."

"Hey, buddy, you got a tissue?" Louis asked Thomas.

"Mom! I'm going to bleed to death!" Her son's voice was edged with hysteria and the dog left her side. She heard Thomas hit the ground, crying, "No, Obi-Wan Kenobi! No!"

"He senses a disturbance in the force," Louis said, amusement in his tone at the dog's name.

He'd made a *Star Wars* reference. Thomas was going to love him. It only figured that her boys would be traitors in this scenario. Louis had that effect on everyone. Everyone but her.

"He's using his Jedi skills to protect you," Louis said.

"I don't want him to!" Thomas yelled.

Hannah scrambled to help him, but the world swirled again when Louis's warm hand vanished from her back.

Why couldn't Thomas have his first real nosebleed on Calvin's watch? Or at school? Somewhere other than here and now?

She forced herself to stand upright so she could take charge. Her vision was gray, but she could get Thomas to the house, pretend she was fine, then take it moment by moment. And not faint. Definitely not faint.

She took a few steps toward him, the tunnel vision returning when she caught sight of his ruined mittens. She bent over.

"Frosty punched me! He punched me and now I'm bleeding. I have to go to the hospital. Mom! *Mom*!"

"Let's get inside," Louis said in a soothing command. "Keep your mitten against your nose. It'll all be okay. It's just a blood vessel that broke and it'll fix itself in seconds. These things are normal."

"But I'm bleeding!"

"Does it hurt?" Louis asked.

There was a pause.

Hannah kept her head down, groping her way toward the house, trying to act natural.

"No," Thomas said with a hint of curiosity.

She needed to get over fainting at the sight of blood. It had completely derailed her life once, and was making it impossible to parent her own child when he needed her now.

Her vision fogged as she tried to navigate the steps to the door. Louis hooked his arm under hers, offering support when she wobbled.

It's just a nosebleed. Everything's okay.

The fog grew worse.

I can handle this. It was nothing! Thomas is fine.

She straightened her spine, determined to shut off this stupid physical reaction, but her vision went dangerously black. Louis practically lifted her up the steps as he said to Thomas, "Boots off. Then find some tissue in the bathroom."

Louis settled her on the bench at the door. But before he followed her son to the bathroom, he remarked, "So you're a mom?"

"Yes."

"And you never did become a doctor, huh?"

* * *

In the kitchen, Hannah gave herself a pep talk, hoping to get rid of that icky feeling in her gut. She hadn't passed out in front of Louis. That was a win.

She could hear him laughing at fart jokes with Thomas in the bathroom, drawing the attention of nine-year-old Wade, who'd been building LEGO in his room. Soon the three of them were cackling together. Apparently males never outgrew their delight with bodily noises.

Listening to their laughter shouldn't warm her heart, especially since Mr. Judgment was not only delighting her sons, but had also just saved the day. He was the last person she ever wanted to owe a thing to.

But she was a mom—a single one at that—and seeing her sons bond with an adult male was like an aphrodisiac. Anyone who could make her boys laugh, and who could turn the tide on an upcoming freak-out, earned a little heart thawing.

Even Louis Bellmore.

There was a thump as small feet hit the bathroom floor, followed by a "There you go, buddy."

Moments later Thomas came ripping around the corner, his socks nearly sliding out from under him on the laminate flooring, his straight brown hair flopping to the side. The dog chased after him with a happy grin.

"Mom! Louis put a cold cloth on the back of my neck and pinched my nose and the nosebleed stopped! Did you know it was just broken blood inside me—"

"A broken blood vessel?" she asked.

"Yeah! And my body is already fixing it."

Hannah smiled, remembering that same feeling of excitement and awe when she'd discovered the curious and very mysterious functioning of the human body around his age.

"It's pretty cool, isn't it, sweetie?"

Both boys had entered the kitchen, their eyes shining at having an unexpected visitor filled with interesting facts, who liked to laugh at the same things they did.

Had it been so long since she and Calvin had laughed together that Louis felt like a marvel?

The sound of the washing machine door closing in the hallway outside the bedrooms was followed by the rush of water. Louis was washing everything that had been soiled so she wouldn't even have to see it.

Another chunk fell off the thawing iceberg in her heart. If Louis wasn't careful he might meet Ms. Sweet-and-Quiet, Gushing-Over-You Hannah, and she had a feeling he preferred her tougher let's-duke-it-out side. Plus she'd never forgive herself if she went sweet around him.

"Louis knows fart *and* diarrhea jokes!" Thomas bounded over to the pantry door and flung it open. "Can I have the new cereal?"

"Sure."

"Really?"

Wade stared at her as if she'd said yes to giving his little brother a Porsche.

Thomas eyed the clock on the stove's console. He knew it was getting close to suppertime. But honestly? Whatever. Hannah felt gross, her body still working through its own fight or flight—or play dead—chemical reaction to the nosebleed, and she didn't have it in her to argue nutrition with her son at the moment.

"Just this once," she warned.

"Best mom ever!" he yelled, hustling to dish himself a snack. Wade rolled his eyes and left the room.

Something cold hit the back of Hannah's neck and she flinched. Louis. She hadn't noticed him approach with a wet facecloth, which he placed on the nape of her neck. Obi nuzzled his soft nose between them, tail wagging.

"Do you have any hard candy?" Louis asked. He was standing close enough that she could feel the heat from his body.

"I have candy! Mom says I can have one piece a day. Can I have one now, Mom?"

"No."

"Your blood sugar likely plummeted," Louis said to her quietly. He was adjusting the cloth, and she wasn't sure if she liked the attention or not. She and Calvin had evolved into "just friends" during their marriage, and it had been a long time since a man had touched her. Not that Louis was crossing lines, but him being close, smelling like the crisp December air, had nudged her into thinking about lines and what it would take to cross one.

She shifted so she was the one holding the cloth.

"Can your mom have one of your candies?" Louis asked Thomas.

"She likes red. Do you want one, too? I have pink, red, blue and green. I ate the yellows and oranges. They're my favorite." Thomas had his bag of candy out, demonstrating his pure, generous spirit.

Louis unwrapped a red one for her. "This'll get you feeling steadier."

"What are you, a doctor?" she asked, a tremor sneaking into her words. He handed her the candy and she popped it in her mouth. It was so sweet it made her cheeks hurt as her salivary glands kicked in.

"Paramedic."

The usual sting of envy hit her in the chest at the medical career choice. "You weren't even that good in biology."

He laughed at her grumbling, which made her feel even more sulky.

"I worked in some remote areas for oil companies after high school. Here in Texas, the UK, Canada, Australia, Saudi Arabia, Holland. You get bored, you move around a lot." He gave her a smile that looked like it was supposed to reassure her of something. It didn't. It reminded her once again that he was still the same old guy he used to be. Never happy staying still. "I gave it up after a few years. You only need to see one major oil and gas disaster before you want out." He shrugged. "Now I fly planes and coach hockey."

Not just any hockey. NHL. The real deal.

The man had already lived more adventures in his thirty-one years than she likely ever would.

Hannah briefly teased herself, imagining what that life might feel like. Exhausting, no doubt. But interesting, for sure.

"You're still pale," he said. "How are your iron levels?"

"I'm fine." She took a deep inhalation, getting a lungful of his aftershave and outdoorsy scent. Man, he smelled good.

"Pregnant?" he whispered.

She let out a bark of laughter, so abrupt it hurt. He knew exactly why she'd almost fainted, and yet here he was, poking and prodding at her and the one unsolvable weakness that had changed her entire life.

Louis gave her shoulder a squeeze in support. She hated it. She loved it. Even though she was still wearing her lightweight puffy jacket she could feel the heat from him as if it had found a tunnel through the lining.

She caught his gaze and realized that even though he'd never said a thing back then, he knew. He understood what had happened on that fateful day in biology class, and why her plans had suddenly zeroed in on marrying Calvin rather than a medical career. One moment with a scalpel had changed her entire future. One thin cut into the amphibian victim and she'd fainted like a maiden whose corset had been done up too tight on a hot day.

April MacFarlane had been freaking out when Hannah regained consciousness, cradled in Louis's arms. Yes, he'd caught her, even though his station had been several over from hers. Because if you're going to humiliate yourself, you might as well go big, right?

She'd immediately started to cry and the teacher had ushered her out of class, assuming she was having some sort of breakdown—which was true. But it had been more than empathy for their dissection victims. She'd known her dream of medical school was over. Through the years her tolerance for wounds of any kind had been slipping. And on that day, in Louis's arms, she realized she was never going to become a doctor, because medical professionals didn't faint when faced with the dissection of a frog. They didn't become light-headed at the sight of blood, like she did. They waded through it all and saved lives without flinching, elbows deep in—

Oh, stop thinking about that!

Hannah had spent the next several months trying anything and everything, from hypnotism and self-talk to watching her hydration and blood sugar levels, to trying the Applied Tension Technique, as well as exposing herself to slasher movies with fake blood squirting everywhere—all in an attempt to alter her fight-or-flight reaction and save her dream career.

Nothing had worked. Eventually she'd had no choice but to throw in the towel, tip up her chin, block out the pain and focus on what she had: Calvin. She'd stopped talking about medical school, and when anyone asked about it she casually said she'd decided she'd rather start a family than spend the next decade in school.

She thought they'd see right through her. But

everyone had agreed, saying how much better it would be to avoid that kind of pressure and expense.

Everyone except Louis. And she'd hated him for it.

* * *

"So you're a pilot?" Hannah asked.

She wouldn't look at him, and was wiping down the kitchen counter even though it didn't need it. The small, cozy house smelled like baking. It was the Hopewells' cabin, one of the older buildings in town, but it had been modernized and was sunny. It felt like a home filled with love.

"Cool!" Thomas exclaimed, looking up from the bowl of cereal he'd been inhaling. "Do you battle starfighters?"

"No," Louis said, not bothering to fight a smile. There was something about the kid's enthusiasm that reminded him of Hannah in high school. Well, before she'd decided to settle for marriage instead of a career. "I mostly just take myself out for jaunts. I used to take tourists for rides, though. But no shooting. No leaving the solar system."

Thomas gave a fake pout. "That sucks."

"Hey," Hannah scolded, giving him a patent mom look that for some crazy reason made Louis feel homesick.

"Nobody ever does anything cool."

"Hey!" Louis protested with a laugh.

Thomas swiped at his milk mustache from drinking the last liquid in his cereal bowl. He bounded up to Louis. "Want to see my *Star Wars* LEGO collection?"

"Put your bowl in the dishwasher, please," Hannah said. "And maybe later. I'm sure Louis has more unpacking to do. Moving is a big job, remember?"

She was looking better now and had more color in her cheeks. She hadn't taken off her jacket, and Louis wondered if she didn't want him to settle in and stay for a visit. Or maybe she was simply eager to get back to hanging her lights.

"We moved here last year," Thomas informed him. "Mom and Dad each got their own house. I have two bedrooms!"

"Wow."

Louis glanced at Hannah, who was rinsing out the cloth. He guessed that she'd put a lot into being a mom and wife, and had to be feeling devastated and a bit lost now.

"Time to go play, Thomas."

The boy slipped from the room and moments later Hannah put a hand on Louis's arm. He glanced at it, unsure what was about to happen. Surely not a kiss. A grateful, you are so wonderful for dealing with my son, his nose, the laundry…

No, she was guiding him out of the kitchen and toward the front door.

"Thank you for your help."

Louis spotted the upright piano in her living room as they passed. He stopped, not wanting to leave. "You still play?"

"Yes."

There was a bottle of wood polish and a rag sitting on top, waiting for her. A half-finished job. Just like the Christmas lights still dangling from her eaves.

He wanted to tell her how she'd inspired him to give music a try after watching her play the piano for kids at the Sweetheart Creek Christmas concert years ago. How he made his own music now, some of which he shared with his hockey players to help soothe their pregame jitters.

"Do you experience low blood pressure?" he asked.

"You can't fix me," she retorted, her voice

edged with annoyance. "I am the way I am, and I'm happy that way."

But she wasn't. He could see the tiredness in her eyes. The sadness. She needed to breathe, have an adventure, do something big for herself.

That wasn't a battle he'd win today, though. He could tell she was gearing up to deflect whatever he said next.

He wanted to tell her that he knew why she hadn't gone to med school. That the way he'd pestered her was about claiming something for herself. Filling her own cup instead of waiting for someone else to notice it needed topping up.

Her hands had gone to her hips, so he sighed and headed to the door before she could shove him out. When he glanced over his shoulder, he noticed she'd backtracked to the kitchen. Louis slipped on his boots, marveling at how small her sons' footwear seemed, sitting beside his.

Hannah reappeared a moment later with a plastic container. "I have something for you."

"For me?"

She shoved it at him, her shoulders drooping as though being nice to him might kill her.

"You look like you want to hook me to an anchor and drop me in the ocean," he said.

"Not a bad idea," she replied lightly, reaching for the doorknob.

He lifted the lid, inspecting the contents. Cookies. Chocolate with something red. They smelled sweet and delicious. And they were in a container she'd want back, not a plastic bag. He had an excuse to see her again.

He grinned. "Thanks. I love cookies."

"Chocolate cherry."

"I really appreciate it."

"They're just cookies." Her cheeks had turned pink.

"We made them," Thomas said, reappearing in a rush. Across the room Wade was leaning in a doorway, watching.

"It's Mom's special recipe," Thomas added.

"It's just a welcome-to-the-neighborhood gift," she said quickly.

"Ah." He met her eyes. "So just being neighborly?"

"It's a…thank-you, too." She swallowed.

He lowered his voice so the boys couldn't hear. "Do I need to worry about poison?"

She gave him a dry look.

As he edged to the door, he asked, "So if you didn't become a doctor, what did you become?"

Was there more to her story than working in the day care and helping out at the boys' school?

"I'm me. Like always." She gave a tight smile and said, "Congrats on your new job."

The door shut briskly behind him and he had a feeling it had taken all of her inner strength not to let it slam.

2

Hannah tried to usher her friend Cassandra McTavish into her house, but the woman was intent on ogling Louis, who was doing something manly with power tools out on his driveway despite the chill of the gray morning.

"Who's the long drink of water next door?" she asked. Hannah rolled her eyes and tugged Obi away from Cass and her five-year-old son.

"Hi, Spaghetti," Dusty said, curling his arms around Obi's neck and receiving a lick on the ear. The kiddo loved the name that Brant Wylder, the local veterinarian and dog rescuer, had given the pooch when he'd found him. To Dusty the dog's name was Spaghetti, and he refused to call him by anything else.

"Put your eyeballs back in your head and get in here," Hannah hissed at her friend, who was still watching Louis.

Cassandra laughed. "He's making you want things, isn't he?" She waved her cowboy hat at him when he looked over, as though sensing he was being talked about. "Mmm. He's yummy all the way from head to toe. Is he single?"

Hannah yanked her inside before she could cause trouble, Dusty and Obi on her heels.

"Hey, how are you feeling, Dusty?" Hannah bent down, studying the small boy. He'd been diagnosed as having a heart issue a few weeks ago, something that had been overlooked since his difficult birth but had recently grown problematic. Cassandra, insistent that her son shouldn't be so small, pale or winded, had pursued the problem until she got his care into the right hands.

The current challenge was the cost of surgery to remedy his condition. Landon, Cass's new boyfriend, wanted to help, but she had reservations about borrowing six figures from the NHL goalie—even for her son. The boy, however, seemed to be running at about half volume compared to usual, and Hannah hoped that Landon would be able to strong-arm her friend into accepting so the surgery could happen soon, and Cass didn't end up buried in debt.

"I saw Dezzie at the hospital," Dusty announced.

"Really? That's so cool." Hannah smiled, knowing that inside the Dragons mascot costume was her friend Violet Granger, who worked for the hockey team.

Thomas came running up, carrying a Batmobile toy in each hand, passing one to Dusty. Her eldest son was nowhere to be seen, which meant he was enjoying his first day of Christmas vacation with his nose in a book or absorbed in a video game Calvin had bought him. Hannah considered calling him out to say hi and play with the other boys, but decided to let him be, knowing her sons were reaching an age where they didn't always want to do the same things, or do them together.

"Quiet play today, please," Hannah warned, nervous that Thomas might tire Dusty out.

"Thanks for letting us stop by," Cassandra said, hanging her farm coat at the door as the boys headed to Thomas's room. She was wearing a red sweater sporting a fuzzy reindeer, complete with a blinking light for a nose. The woman was as into Christmas as Hannah was. In fact, she was even selling beautiful Christmas trees out at her ranch to make a little extra holiday cash. "Dusty's been going stir-crazy out there."

"I thought Rylnn was spending more time out at your place," Hannah said, referring to Landon's young daughter. Landon and Cass were pretty new as a couple, but seemed to be blending their families fairly well. It gave Hannah hope that if she found someone for herself it would be just as seamless.

"She's so girlie Dusty tends to go a bit crazy after playing with her for days on end."

"Alexa needs to adopt some boys Dusty's age." Cass's sister lived just down the road, but so far she and her husband didn't have kids.

"Cash is on board, but I don't think Alexa's ready."

The women moved toward the kitchen and Hannah tipped her head in the direction the boys had gone. "How is he?"

"Good. There's no rush for the surgery other than the fact that I want to see him strong as soon as possible."

"If there's anything I can do, let me know."

"Thanks. Hey, did you hear the news? Polly's

expecting!" Her sister's hired hand, Nick Wylder, and his girlfriend, Polly, lived next door on Alexa's ranch.

"That's great!"

"April's planning a baby shower for her."

"I heard a rumor we may need to plan a shower for April, too." Everyone in town was having babies, it seemed. Hannah hoped her cousin Athena and her sister put in a baby section in the shop they planned to open next month. "Maybe one for you, too?" She waggled her brows at Cass, who laughed.

"Yeah, we're not going there."

"I thought things were good with Landon."

"They are. But no. We're not doing the whole…thing." She scrunched her nose and Hannah let it go, curious as to why kids seemed to be off the table. Then again, she hadn't even seen Cass and Landon kiss or hold hands yet, so maybe it was too soon to start talking babies. She just hoped the two single parents weren't using each other as parenting pinch-hitters to make their lives easier, and giving up on love in the process.

Although she could definitely see the appeal of bringing in a pinch-hitter—especially since they both had busy lives and neither had their baby-daddy or baby-mommy in the picture.

In the kitchen, Hannah turned on the coffeemaker, then the kettle, and leaned against the counter." I heard you two are going to the Dragons' Christmas gala on Friday."

"Yup."

"Do you have your dress yet?" Hannah could imagine the black tie affair, the dresses that Cass and her friends Violet and Daisy-Mae planned on wearing. They'd be gorgeous. Hanging out with NHL stars in a beautiful ballroom. It was all so far away from the life Hannah lived that she wanted to soak up every detail.

"Yup. We'll have to find you a date for next year."

Hannah laughed. A date? She could be living in France by then if Calvin liked what he saw when he met with the engineering firm that was calling him over there for meetings. The deal was that if the job looked good the whole family would move so they could still be geographically close to each other. It was an exhausting thought, but she wanted Calvin in her boys' lives and would do whatever it took.

"Find you a yummy hockey player," Cass added.

Hannah waved a hand. "Men just complicate things."

"You're not looking to date again?"

"I have the boys. I'm busy enough."

"They'll grow up faster than you think. You're going to need more than a dog to fill that hole."

Hannah felt a pang at the idea of her sons leaving the nest. "Then I'll get a second dog."

Cass didn't laugh. "The boys are going to be on a different continent for almost a full week. When do they go? Tomorrow?" Hannah nodded. "Their lives are already becoming separate from yours."

Seriously. Did her friend know her every sore spot?

Hannah fiddled with the sugar bowl in the middle of the table. Wade and Thomas were tagging along with Calvin and their grandmother on the trip to Paris. The four were making an official vacation of it, with a planned stop at Disneyland Paris. The boys were going to bond even more deeply with their dad, which had always been a secret wish of Hannah's. And yet she had reservations, too, as though she feared being replaced in their hearts, or that she might not be able to keep up with the excitement and adventures Calvin was able to provide. She wanted to be there for her children, create stability and consistency in their lives, but she also didn't want to be boring.

"You don't want to move there, do you?" Cass asked.

"Oh," Hannah said, waving her hand again. "You know me. I'm happy in Sweetheart Creek, but family comes first. I'm sure France will be an incredible experience for all of us if it comes to that."

The front door opened and a woman called out, "I hope y'all didn't start without me." Obi scrambled to his feet, let out a bark and careened out of the kitchen to go check out the visitor.

Cassandra called, "Perfect timing, Athena! The coffee's ready."

"So's the tea!" Hannah added.

"Bet she chooses coffee," Cass whispered.

"She likes tea."

"Yeah, but she's burning the candle on both ends at the moment with her job and trying to open the shop next month. It's gonna be coffee." She lifted her voice and called out, "I'm just nagging Hannah about speaking up for what she wants."

Cassandra stood, sloshing dark coffee into the red-and-white cup Thomas had painted for Hannah on Mother's Day—a thoughtful gift arranged by his teacher. Then she poured hot water from the kettle into the teapot, filling the room with the scent of chocolate chai, Hannah's favorite.

"Hannah, listen to Cassandra," Athena Gavras ordered, followed by the resounding thunk of her cowboy boots hitting the mat at the door. "Who's the hottie next door? Is he the reason for this conversation about speaking up for what you want?"

Hannah choked on a fake laugh. "It's Louis."

Since her cousin worked for the Dragons NHL team in San Antonio, like Louis, but as their dietician, she should have recognized him.

"Because I can see why you'd want that hunk of hotness, even though jocks aren't my type," Athena said, entering the room while unwinding a stylist, rose-colored scarf that brought out the cheerful pink highlights in her dark brown hair. "So if you're trying to summon the courage to request some adult time with him, I totally back up Cass. Although he looks an awful lot like Louis Bellmore from a distance, don't you think?"

"He *is* Louis Bellmore," Hannah grumbled, as Cass handed her a cup of chai. "Thanks."

Athena began laughing. "I assumed my eyes were lying and that it couldn't be him. I mean...next door? To you?" She laughed again. "How is he even still alive?"

"Apparently looks don't kill," Hannah said mildly.

"Well, if you need help hiding his body, I've been eavesdropping on the mystery novel book club that meets in the bookstore near the arena, and I might have a few suggestions."

"I'm not going to kill the man," Hannah muttered into her cup.

Maybe her spats with Louis had been more legendary than she'd realized if Athena still remembered her ranting about him. Then again, Sweetheart Creek had never gone light on gossip, and him being back in town was no doubt stirring up old stories.

"We were talking about Paris," Cass announced, pushing the red cup closer to Athena. "I assume you want coffee?"

"Yes, please!" She grabbed the mug and raised it to her lips.

Cass shot Hannah a look of triumph. Hannah stuck out her tongue, realizing that maybe Thomas was picking up habits from her, not Wade.

"Hannah doesn't want to go," Cass said, sitting again.

"I said I'll go to France," Hannah protested.

"But you never said you *want* to go."

"Let's change the subject, please."

Cass's voice grew slightly dreamy. "Isn't Louis lovely? He's that perfect blend of strong but not bulky, you know?"

"Not my type. I'm looking for a nerdy professor." Athena turned to Hannah. "I brought you this from the store's latest shipment." She handed her a book. "It made me think of you. It's an autobiography about a woman who changes her entire life after divorce, and basically goes out and kicks butt."

"Inspiration, perhaps?" Cassandra asked, snagging the book to read the dust jacket. "Did she move to Paris to follow her ex? Because that doesn't sound like butt kicking." She gave Hannah a meaningful look.

Hannah sighed. "I'm not *following* him. It'll be an enriching experience for all of us." She stole the book back.

"So have you told Louis how awful he is?" Athena asked, a devilish smile peeking above the rim of her cup.

"Of course I have." She tucked a strand of her shoulder-length hair back into its bun.

Athena said to Cassandra, pointing at Hannah

with her thumb, "This crazy woman used to pick on him *every day* in school."

"He always started it," she mumbled.

Her cousin gave her a smug, knowing smile. "I figured you had a crush on him or something. I kept wondering when you'd give up the fight and kiss him. I mean, every girl in town was crushing on him when he moved here."

"Not me!"

"So? Has he asked you out yet?" Athena asked.

"Why would he?" Hannah asked, crossing her arms. "And I don't know why you're both so interested in this. He was awful in high school and I never had a crush on him. And I never will."

"He's always had this protective vibe around you," Athena stated, "like he was some sort of Neanderthal who wanted to drag you back to his cave and kiss you."

"You need to get out more," Hannah said, trying to ignore the shivers that zipped through her body at the thought of Louis kissing her. She'd bet his kisses were divine.

Except for the whole it-being-Louis thing.

"Maybe try reading fewer caveman romance novels," Cassandra suggested to Athena.

"That's not a genre," she protested. She grinned. "But it should be."

"I bet it is," Cass said. "You should look it up."

"Remind me if I forget. I'll stock a few in the new store and recommend them to Mrs. Fisher. I bet she'd get a kick out of them."

While they talked books, Hannah tried to imagine finding love again—with someone other than Louis. She adored Hallmark movies, where the characters always got swept up in sweet love, and the complications in their lives just sort of resolved and fell away without much pain. Was real love like that? Kind of like what she and Calvin had started out with, but with some staying power and a lot more kick?

Hannah sighed. She and Calvin had never seemed to quite find that spark she saw in the movies, and when they'd separated he'd questioned if they'd ever truly been in love.

It had felt like love to her.

Was it because they'd been so young that it had felt not quite real to him? Or had he truly not fallen for her? If she'd been more adventurous would he have stayed interested? Or was she simply comparing real life to the fictional, feel-good dreams that were sold by movie companies?

"The only thing that Louis has ever done," Hannah said firmly, hoping to put the subject to bed once and for all, "is pick apart my life and make me feel like I'm not living up to my potential. He acts like his life goals are superior and that wanting a family is boring."

The heat of anger had returned. He'd really managed to get under her skin all those years ago, and then had stirred it all up again the day before yesterday, as though she'd never been able to grow up and move past it.

Athena waved away Hannah's argument. "You're single. And from what I've heard, Louis is, too."

"You know," Cassandra said, "the man might have a point about the family thing. There *is* more to life than simply raising our sweet little hellions."

"There are also several good reasons why Louis is still single," Hannah stated, locking her hands around her cup. His personality being the big one.

"But he's hot," Cass said, sighing wistfully.

"And he's smart." Athena lifted a brow. "Accomplished. Does he read? I've always been a sucker for a reader."

"He's bossy," Hannah countered. "He thinks he has the right to dictate what I do with my life."

"Just like Calvin," her cousin muttered.

"We *discuss* things," Hannah argued. Calvin

had a say in her life, but he didn't run the entire show.

"I never saw that bossy side of Louis," Athena mused. "I only saw the two of you flirting—sorry, verbally attacking each other—around town."

"Has he really made you feel less than worthy?" Cassandra asked, tipping her head to the side and sending her curls into a tangle.

"Well..." Hannah fumbled for something concrete to support her claims. "He..." He'd been nothing short of awesome with Thomas the other day.

But she knew what he was like, deep down. She knew what his judgment felt like, and that if she waited long enough it would pop up and blindside her.

"He carried Mom inside when she fainted," Thomas called from the hall outside his room, "and he fixed my nosebleed."

The little eavesdropper. Seriously. Heat was already creeping up Hannah's face as she tried to figure out how to explain the incident, while her friends gaped at her.

"It wasn't like that," she said numbly.

"You were holding out on us?" Cassandra shot her an unimpressed look.

"It's the quiet ones," Athena said knowingly.

She had leaned back, legs crossed, her coffee mug secured between her elegant hands.

"He didn't *carry* me."

"Wait," Athena added. "Do you still have that thing about blood?"

"What thing?" Cassandra asked.

"I tend to get woozy when I see blood, even though everything's totally fine." Hannah closed her eyes, trying to erase the image of Thomas's nose and mittens.

"It's why she didn't become a doctor," Athena stated.

Hannah's eyes flew open. "You know about that?"

She shrugged. "I figured it out a few years ago. At first I thought dissecting the frog was an isolated incident. Because you were still totally fascinated and jumped right back into science—as long as you didn't have to dissect anything." She turned to Cass. "Louis caught her when she fainted in class."

"No!" Cassandra breathed.

"I thought she was finally going to see Louis's attention for what it really was, and date him instead of Calvin."

"Wh-what?" Hannah sputtered. "I do *not* like Louis Bellmore. I have *never* liked him. And—and he never…" He had caught her, though. Like a hero. An annoying hero who wasn't supposed to have even noticed her during the worst moment of her life.

"So he had to carry you yesterday?" Cassandra asked, leaning forward, a fist tucked under her chin. "Like, to your room?" Her grin was almost evil.

"I just leaned on him, and then he put a wet cloth on the back of my neck and gave me a candy to bring my blood sugar back up." She began talking faster, worried they'd think the situation had actually meant something. Which it hadn't. But it felt like it could if she wasn't careful. "And he ran all of Thomas's things through the wash after getting him cleaned up."

Realizing she was twisting a tendril of hair around her finger, she dropped her hands, locking them around her cup once again.

Cassandra had a far-off expression that probably wasn't too different from her own. Single moms had two kinds of fantasies. The first she called Hot Men Scenarios. They were the standard sweep-you-up, real-life-doesn't-exist ones. And then there were Thoughtful Hot Men Fantasies, where the guy runs loads of laundry while cleaning the entire house and making you dinner.

Preferably something that didn't come out of a box or can.

Both were enough to send a woman off to la-la land for considerable amounts of time.

Kind of like the little fantasy playing out in her mind right now. Louis was wrangling with Thomas's mattress, getting the fitted sheet put on in a way that stayed when a bouncing boy climbed—actually bounded—into bed each night.

"You have a crush!" Athena giggled.

"I do not!"

"So totally do," Cassandra said with a small smile. "And who can blame you?"

"Maybe I'll have to develop a fainting condition." Athena winked at her. "That seems like a good way to catch a man around here."

Hannah gave an exasperated sigh while her cousin laughed.

Someone knocked on the front door, then it swung open and a male voice called out, "Knock, knock! Just returning your cookie container."

Seriously. Louis Bellmore had the worst timing in the world.

* * *

Louis made himself at home in Hannah's kitchen even though he could tell she didn't particularly want him there. Her friends, however, were so curious he could practically feel the energy crackling in the air. He knew Athena, of course, the team's dietician and Hannah's cousin. The gal with the wild brown curls he was pretty certain was the woman his goalie, Landon Jackson, was using as his nanny or was dating or something. Honestly, there weren't enough hours in the day to keep up with his players and their love lives.

He nodded at Athena, then said to the new gal, "I'm Louis, Hannah's neighbor."

"Cassandra." She gave him a firm handshake, with a no-nonsense look that brought up a strong urge to salute her. Then she popped up and reached for the largest cup in the cupboard. "Want coffee?"

He sniffed the air. Cinnamon and spice… "Actually, is that chai tea I smell?"

Cassandra's smile grew. "A whole pot for the taking." She lifted it and poured him a cup. "Honey? Milk?"

"Yes, please. Although, really, I should probably go..."

"Just how Hannah takes hers." Cassandra

practically pushed him into a chair next to Hannah. It looked like he was staying.

Thomas raced in with a gigantic smile as Louis doctored his beverage.

"Hey, kid. How are your intergalactic missions going today?"

"I destroyed some drones!" Thomas held out a fist, and Louis gave it a bump while taking a gulp of his tea.

He finally allowed himself to glance at Hannah. She was watching with what seemed like a mixture of warmth and disgust. He set the empty cookie container in the middle of the table. "Thanks for the *neighborly* gift. Your cookies were amazing."

Her cheeks turned pink. She looked cute today, with her wavy brown hair pulled into a loose knot and wearing a baggy sweater that hugged the lovely curves motherhood had given her.

"Athena!" Thomas declared, jostling Louis from his thoughts. "Do you have any new books about galaxies? I want to read about Tatooine! It's where Luke Skywalker is from."

"Why would you have a book about galaxies?" Louis asked her. He'd known the dietician vaguely in high school. Their paths crossed in a few meetings and here and there at work, but he was in the dark about her personal life. Although he knew she'd published a few cookbooks and that she was Hannah's cousin—a fact that had almost caused him to ask about her on multiple occasions. But as far as Louis knew, Athena didn't have kids of her own, and didn't look as if she might be a *Star Wars* superfan.

She shrugged. "Just a project my sister and I are working on."

"She's opening a bookstore in Sweetheart Creek!" Thomas exclaimed.

"Really?" Louis felt a flash of alarm. Was she quitting the Dragons? He needed the best professionals Miranda Fairchild could hire. They were making strides this season as a new team with a lot of older players, but losing the woman who nagged them about proper nutrition wouldn't help move them forward to more wins.

"Tatooine is a fictional planet, Thomas," Hannah said. "It's not real."

"I know." His focus was fixed on Athena, who hummed thoughtfully.

"There are a lot of interesting books about *Star Wars,* and I have a new shipment coming early next week," she told him. "I'll text your mom if there's anything good in there, okay?"

"Okay! Thanks!" He scooted off again, hollering, "Dusty! I'm getting new *Star Wars* books!"

Hannah winced at her cousin, who laughed and told her not to worry about it, then turned her attention to Louis. "I'd heard a dirty rumor you'd moved back to town."

"Yeah, I did. What's this side hustle? You quitting the team?"

"Nope."

"Good."

"I heard you're a pilot now?" Athena said. "Any chance you could fly me to work sometimes? I hate mornings."

Louis laughed. "I'm pretty sure half the team is moving out here. Seems like the place to be. But yeah, I might be able to help you with the commute now and again."

Hannah was watching him, arms crossed, her tea abandoned. She looked...jealous? No, that couldn't be. Miffed, maybe.

"He doesn't fight with starfighters," Thomas interjected, sliding in from the other room. "He stays in this galaxy."

"Thanks!" Athena said. "I was wondering about that."

The kid nodded and dashed out again. He was

a ball of energy and Louis had no idea how Hannah kept up with him.

"What have you ladies been up to?" he asked.

Hannah had lifted her cup to her lips, reminding him how entirely kissable they looked. "Cassandra's selling Christmas trees if you need one."

"I do, actually. Well, no. I don't actually decorate. But if I did I'd need a tree."

"Scrooge," Hannah muttered.

"If I'm Scrooge, then you're Will Ferrell in the movie *Elf.*"

"Hardly."

"Do you have kids?" Cassandra asked. "Hannah works in the day care down the street, Colts and Fillies. It's the best."

Louis glanced at Hannah, who was watching him, jaw clenched. She thought he was going to judge her for the fact that her job didn't pay well and likely had no benefits, he knew.

So much wasted potential.

But there was no way he'd say so. He wouldn't give her the satisfaction of a fight.

"Full-time?" he asked.

"Half."

"Do the boys go there?"

"They're in school."

"You're going to ask for full-time, though, right?" Cassandra pressed.

"Edith had to make additional cuts." Hannah sounded glum, even though she'd pasted that stupid I'm-happy-don't-worry-about-me smile on her face. "It's fine, though. Tonya really needed the extra hours this month. She doesn't get much in the way of child support, and Calvin takes good care of us."

Her glance darted Louis's way, but he kept his mouth shut.

"Those boys are going to grow up one day, then where will you be financially?" Cassandra muttered in warning, before taking another sip of her coffee.

Louis liked this gal. No wonder his goalie was so smitten with her.

"I heard you went to college," he said to Hannah, leaning an elbow on the table.

"I took a few early childhood education classes."

"For a teaching degree?" He felt a moment of hope that she'd managed to use her smarts and stand up for what she wanted, instead of being so agreeable that she got passed over both professionally and with Calvin. Maybe she had something to fall back on and Louis could quit worrying about her.

She shook her head and looked away.

"Do you ever think about expanding your... uh, career?"

She sighed heavily, as if she knew what he was thinking.

"You should upgrade your education and become a teacher!" Athena said, laying her palms on the table. "Say goodbye to that day care. You'd be an awesome teacher."

"Hear, hear!" Cassandra declared.

"Goodbye to changing diapers and wiping drool," her cousin stated.

"Goodbye to poor pay and not enough hours," her friend added.

"I need that flexibility," Hannah insisted.

"You don't," Cassandra said. "You need a retirement fund. Us single moms need to look out for number one and build our own security. You thought you and Calvin would be a team forever. But you're not. You need options."

"You don't need nearly as much flexibility now that the boys are in school," Athena said, "And when you do, the almighty Calvin can leave work early or even stay home when the boys are sick."

Louis found himself nodding, and quickly stopped.

"I don't have the time, money or focus right now," Hannah said. "Things work with me being at the day care. And it's local, where we all live. School would mean being in the city again."

Despite her protests, Louis could see it. They'd stirred up her desire to want more, and it was a dangerous, slippery slope. But that spark of fight in her eyes, even though she was trying to tamp it down, was sexy.

"I bet some of your classes could be applied toward a teaching degree," he said. "That would cut down on time and cost. You also might be able to take some of the courses online. And..." he sucked in a deep breath "...even though this offer might lead to my murder, I could fly you to some of your classes."

Fly her to classes.

Seriously.

Was Louis trying to prove how wonderful his life was in comparison to hers, or was he thinking that showing off like some sexy jet-set hero was going to make her heart flutter?

All the man had to do was walk into a room and suddenly Hannah's life was being turned upside down and Louis had her friends telling her that how she was living wasn't good enough for her and her sons. The worst part was that they made a valid argument, and had stirred up an urge to reach a little higher and find something better for herself.

Hannah needed to lock that urge down. She'd worked really hard over the past year and a half to smooth over the disturbance of the divorce and resettle the boys.

"I know a guy in admissions at the college in San Antonio." Athena was already tapping out a message on her phone. "I'm going to ask him about how to upgrade your early childhood development classes into a teaching degree."

"Ask how much she can do off-campus," Louis told her. Athena nodded and continued to type.

"Y'all, this is nice. Really," Hannah said carefully, hoping to curb their efforts before they literally marched her off to college.

"I'll ask if you have to do any practicums and if you could do them here in town," Athena added, not looking up from her phone. "Naina Elm at the elementary school takes education students all the time and she'd take Hannah in a heartbeat. Whenever I see her at the library she's always talking about how much her daughter, Anya, loves her."

"Really, I'm sure I can look into this *if* I become interested," Hannah said. "You don't need to bother your friend, or Naina." She desperately wanted to pull Athena's phone from her grip and hide it.

"She won't look it up," Cassandra whispered, reaching out to tap the table in front of Athena. "Send the message."

"Hey, that's not fair! My life has been in turmoil. Can't I just enjoy some calm before someone creates a new storm?"

The telltale sound of a text being sent filled the air.

All. Louis's. Fault.

She really was going to murder him.

Louis winced when he noted Hannah's expression. They were pushing her too hard, too fast. He could see she wanted to become a teacher, but there were so many obstacles, and they were overwhelming her.

As far as he was concerned, it was her time to

shine as brightly as the sun on a cloudless day. But she needed time and space to work through the barriers and wrap her mind around the career change.

"So what are y'all doing for Christmas?" he asked, knowing she loved the holidays.

"Oh! The piano in the barn needs tuning," Hannah said, clapping her hands together. "Does anyone know of a local tuner? The one who did mine after we moved cost me an arm and a leg."

"Must be difficult playing now," Louis said dryly, earning a chuckle from Cassandra.

"Wise guy," she murmured with a smile, and he caught Hannah flashing her a look.

"The kids' Christmas concert is coming up," Hannah explained, "and the barn's piano is horribly out of tune. Nobody'll be able to sing on key if I can't get that thing back in shape."

"You're accompanying the singers?" Louis asked, perking up.

She nodded.

"Are you going to come?" Athena asked him.

"I'm sure you'll be busy, given your hockey schedule," Hannah stated quickly.

He shrugged. "I'll probably have a game or late practice."

"We have some days off around Christmas,

Louis," Athena said, her tone dry as though she was busting him in a lie. "Come listen to the little kiddos sing out of tune. It's cute."

"Maybe I will." He'd like to see Hannah perform, if he was free that day. In high school she'd played the piano while the kids sang, and there had been something about the way she'd become swept up in the music that had led him to learn guitar, piano and a few other instruments. He loved putting sounds together and had recently begun creating sound baths for his players, to help them settle and focus before a game.

"Yeah, well, if you come, don't lurk at the back and stare at me like you did in high school," Hannah grumbled.

Louis swallowed. She'd noticed him? He'd left before she'd finished her performance, worried that she'd track him down and demand to know what he was doing there. A high school kid at a children's concert, watching the singing, having snacks and waiting for Santa to appear with some presents... Yeah, it looked weird. He'd gone out of curiosity and had been enthralled by her hidden musical talent.

"Fine. I'll sit in a seat. And I can tune a piano," he added, immediately wondering why on earth he'd said that.

They all faced him.

"What?" Hannah asked softly.

"I rented a room from a piano tuner when I was taking my paramedic courses. I can probably get it sounding okay if it's not too far out of whack."

"You're hired!" Cassandra exclaimed. She dug around in her jeans pocket. "In fact, I happen to have the key for the barn right here. I was dropping off a tree earlier. I'll let Mrs. Fisher know you and Hannah have the key. Feel free to tune it at your leisure—as long as you have the key back to her by the end of her shift today."

Hannah took the horseshoe key chain and handed it to Louis, being careful not to touch him in the process.

He shook his head. "I need someone to come with me."

"Why?" Hannah asked. "You've forgotten where the community barn is?"

He remembered. It was a gorgeous old structure that had been converted into a community hall, just outside of town. You tended to remember places where you felt your life change.

"No," he said slowly. "I need someone to tell me if my tuning is up to her royal specifications." He took Hannah's hand, and she inhaled sharply as he gave her back the key, folding her fingers around it.

Her gaze was steely as she looked at him. Yeah, once again he should probably fear for his life. He was poking his nose in her business and she didn't like that. It probably didn't help that her friends seemed to be on his side.

"My royal specifications aren't part of tuning a piano," she said, sounding a bit breathless.

"I toy with the piano, but mostly stick to guitar. I'm not an expert like you are."

"Mr. Adventure," she said. Yup. There it was. The Great Wall of Hannah Murphy, keeping him out with one simple nickname that erased his fantasy of the two of them playing a song together in her living room, laughing, smiling and sharing a moment. "You probably learned just a few bars from "Stairway to Heaven" to impress a chick, and now tell everyone you can play."

"Better than putting routine before living life," he snapped back. The woman was so hung up on stability that she'd never let her guard down long enough to see him for who he really was, for the potential he had to offer. They'd never have a jam session in her living room.

She glowered, and he cursed himself for reacting to her barbs.

"I doubt we could even get a professional in this close to Christmas," Athena was saying, ignoring their bickering. "Y'all better get down there."

"Together," Cassandra added.

Had Louis ever mentioned how much he liked Hannah's friends?

"Now?" Hannah clutched her cup like it could protect her.

"Now," Athena confirmed.

"We'll babysit," Cassandra offered.

"We only have the key until five," Athena said.

"We can borrow it another day. Maybe on the weekend. I'm sure Louis is—"

"No time like the present," he interrupted, standing up. "I've got two away games this weekend." He gave a quick nod of goodbye to Athena and Cassandra.

"Always the bossy pants," Hannah grumbled as he ushered her to the door, his hand against her lower back.

When she didn't jump away he felt a stirring of hope. He felt like he'd been making progress with her earlier, and even though he hadn't been able to keep his mouth shut and had annoyed her, he wanted to believe that they were on the path to friendship.

3

Louis had announced that he would drive, and Hannah hunched down in the cab of his truck, marveling at all the upgrades it had. His vehicle was a thing of beauty.

The silence was awkward as he drove them through Sweetheart Creek and out of town to where the community center was located. But maybe it was good they didn't speak. Hannah wasn't exactly impressed with how they'd all ganged up on her about becoming a teacher. While the career's financial security was tempting, it was a big idea to take in.

Truthfully, Hannah hadn't expected a divorce. She'd believed she and Calvin would be a team forever, and that the time to do something big with her life would eventually come along if she was just patient enough. And sure, maybe she should have pressed harder to complete her own degree. But she'd helped Calvin get his by working reception at a dealership while raising Wade, and by the time Thomas came along, the dream of returning to school had just felt like more work.

Going back to school *would* be a lot of work—even if they stayed stateside and didn't move to Paris. Taking classes, working, teaching piano and caring for the boys during her week with them would take a toll on all of them.

"Well, here we are," she said, breaking the silence as they approached the hall. Freshly painted in a classic red, with pastures stretching out around it, the old barn look almost majestic. As Hannah fiddled with the giant door's lock she inhaled the aromas of home—dry country air filled with the scents of earth, and growing things. It was a simpler life. Today there was something new and equally wonderful in the air and Hannah inhaled again, trying to identify its origin.

With a jolt she realized it was Louis.

Hannah let them into the building, where dim light sifted through a few side windows in faded streams. Partially blind from being out in the bright sunshine, she fumbled along the wall for the light switches, until she bumped into something solid. Louis.

He mumbled an apology while she struggled to recall how to draw a breath. Tingles shot down to her toes when he pressed a hand to her back, reaching around her with his other one to hit the lights. They flickered a few times before illuminating the large, open space, exposed rafters and partial hayloft that was now an upstairs office.

Trapped for a moment between Louis and the wall, Hannah found herself curious about who this man really was. One thing she'd learned working at Colts and Fillies was that everyone behaved the way they did for a reason. Everyone had a story and a history, even when only a few years old. And that story impacted their choices and the way they behaved. She knew that held true for Louis, who'd moved here as a teen, then left, like her. And now he was back.

But why? And why now?

"How long are you here for this time, Louis?"

He still hadn't stepped away from her, and his blue eyes dropped to meet hers. "As long as I'm wanted."

By whom?

"And after? Where will you go? To the city?"

she asked, curious if hockey was the pulling force that brought him places, the way her family had drawn her back to Sweetheart Creek.

He shrugged. "We'll see." Then he sidestepped, heading toward the old upright piano located at the back of the barn near a short platform that served as a stage. Around it, a few square straw bales had been artfully placed as decorations, in case the wooden walls and rough plank flooring didn't create enough ambiance.

"How are your parents?" he asked.

"Still the happiest married couple I've ever known."

He chuckled as he tugged the bench away from the piano. "Why do you say that with disgust?"

"I did not. I'm happy for them."

"No, there was definite disgust."

"Okay, fine," she admitted with a sigh. "Maybe. But seriously? Are they faking it? They make it look so easy."

Louis hooked his hands around the piano and, before Hannah could jump in to help him, pulled it away from the wall. The wheels squealed and protested as he strong-armed it to the spot he wanted so he could step behind it to work. That man was strong. Yummy.

Hannah cleared her throat and examined the instrument. It looked older than she recalled. Dustier, too. She swiped a hand over the bench, then coughed as she dusted her hands, reminding herself to fill Wade with antihistamines before the concert so he didn't sneeze the entire night.

Louis glanced over his shoulder as he lifted the lid protecting the piano keys, then experimentally pressed a few, proving the instrument did indeed sound awful. "Maybe if you find the right person it *is* that easy," he finally replied.

"And what would either of us know about that?" she asked with a laugh. The nice thing about Louis was that she never worried about hurting his feelings. She could be blunt and to the point with him.

"Maybe we just need to open our minds." He opened the top of the piano, hinges creaking as he sent Hannah one of those carefree, casual smiles that were kind of sexy if she let herself think about it. Which she would not. Ever.

"Open our minds to what? Possibilities?"

"I'm sure there are lots of eligible, single men in Sweetheart Creek."

"I'm *not* going to date Henry Wylder."

Louis laughed. "That guy's still around? He must be in his hundreds by now."

"He's not as old as you'd think." She wasn't sure Henry had even hit eighty yet. "Anyway, even if I got over the age thing, he's way too much of an old grump for me."

"I thought you liked grumps?"

She placed her hands under her chin and batted her eyelashes. "He'd be the storm cloud to my sunny disposition. A true opposites-attract romance."

Louis choked on a laugh and she smiled. Sometimes the two of them just…connected. Not always, but when they did it felt incredible. Like her heart was opening with joy, or something equally cheesy and very un-Louis-like.

The man was like one of those chocolate eggs her boys loved. You never knew what was hidden inside, sometimes a toy, sometimes a puzzle.

And Louis was often the puzzle when she'd been hoping for a toy. But sometimes he brought laughter when she was expecting a fight, kind of like right now, so she supposed it all evened out in the end.

The man prodded her and made her think even when she didn't want to. But maybe it wasn't for the reasons she'd always assumed.

He had a good sense of how far he could go, and often stopped just before she snapped.

It was infuriating, and she often found herself wishing he was more like Calvin—straightforward and easy to predict. Her ex was linear, like a marble rolling down a tube. Louis, on the other hand, was as predictable as a bouncy ball operating under zero gravity after a crazed preschooler gave it a good chucking.

Like now. Could he even tune a piano? And if he could, was there anything this man *couldn't* do? How had he fit so much living into his thirty-one years?

Then again, she was fairly confident he was bluffing about his skills, because when they'd hopped into his truck she'd asked if he wanted to grab his tools for tuning the piano. He'd just patted his pocket and announced that he was all set. Every piano tuner she knew arrived with a duffel bag.

Hannah dropped down onto the dusty bench and started running her fingers up and down the keys. There was a vibration on Middle D that shouldn't be there.

Louis, who was still peering inside the piano, gave a low whistle.

"What?"

"There are a lot of strings in here."

"Do you know what you're doing?" she asked, hitting a few more keys.

"Ouch! Stop that."

"Sorry." Hannah sat on her hands so she wouldn't be tempted to knock his fingers with the internal hammers that hit the strings he was studying. All eighty-eight keys were covered in a layer of grime from a year of disuse. Off to the right a C key wasn't sitting properly. Bringing the instrument up to a reasonable standard was going to take not only time, but skill—something she was certain Louis didn't possess.

"There's a high C looking odd. How does it look in there?" she asked.

"Which one?"

"Are your fingers clear?"

"Yes."

Hannah stretched her neck up to peek at him. He was doing something on his phone instead of looking inside the instrument.

"What are you doing? Researching how to tune a piano or texting your girlfriend?"

He gave her a saucy glance, and she couldn't decide whether that meant yes, he was researching the job, or he was texting a woman.

She tapped and wiggled the funny key, which remained silent. She needed that one for "Here

Comes Santa Claus," the song the kids all sang together at the end to bring out Santa and his bag of gifts. "What's up with this key?"

He bent forward again. "Wire broke. We can probably bring it back to life if we use a little care. Bring out this old beast's potential."

"Honestly, I don't know if it can be salvaged." She must have been overly optimistic when she'd looked at it last month.

Hannah ran her fingers down the keys, caressing them like they were old friends. When she was a kid this had simply been a piano. She'd sat down, played her music, got up again. But looking at it now, with its chipped and yellowed keys, she realized that as dear and familiar as it was, the past few years of neglect and abuse were showing. This old barn in Texas wasn't exactly climate controlled, and the instrument's precious inner workings were likely cracked and warped from years spent in the dry heat of the dusty countryside. It was time to have the instrument replaced. And like the idea of going back to school, there was no room in the budget.

Louis watched Hannah over the top of the piano. She seemed resigned to disappointment. Was it the state of the instrument or the fact that she was twigging on to the fact that he didn't have a clue about tuning pianos? He'd figured with his musical ear he could sort it out, but once he'd opened the lid he'd realized it was a lot trickier than sorting out a six-string guitar.

"What are you thinking?" he asked.

"I don't know yet."

"Is there money for a new piano?"

She shook her head.

"Think we can squeeze another season out of this thing?" It would be a shame if she didn't get to play in the community concert. She was good, and he'd loved seeing her shine when she performed. Granted, he hadn't heard her play since a teen, but seeing as she had a piano at home, taught lessons and was looking at this one with sadness and longing, he had a feeling music was still a big part of her life.

He closed the piano, then set his pocket knife on top.

Hannah's gaze locked onto its beat-up red handle, a strange expression of recognition flitting across her face before she quickly looked away.

She remembered the knife. A gift that went everywhere with him.

She might never know how special it was to him, and that was okay. She might think he'd held on to it for all these years because it was a handy tool. But maybe one day she'd realize he'd kept it because it was from her, and it mattered most because of that.

"We need to find you a new piano," he announced. "Where should we start looking?"

"I didn't say it needs replacing right now," she snapped. "Quit trying to solve problems that aren't yours."

Louis met her eyes, and it felt like a thread of history was dangling between them, tangling the past with the present. Louis found himself wishing he could back off and let everything be. Let life be simple, the way she wanted it.

But he couldn't.

And she knew that, too.

"This will do for another year. It just needs tuning." She ran her fingers down the out-of-tune keys again, hitting the dead one and leaving a gap in the notes ringing through the empty building.

Louis raised his hands in surrender. "Just trying to be helpful."

He eyed Hannah, considering her as well as

his next move. Why she fought so hard to stay safe was a mystery to him.

She locked her gaze on his even though he could tell it made her uncomfortable. "Don't try and sort me out," she said.

"I'm not."

"Then quit staring, and tell me this piano will work for the concert."

"You want me to tell you that we can make it sound good? That it won't be an embarrassment to your skills? That the town won't think you lost your musical touch when you play on this thing?"

She crossed her arms, a sign the fight was rising inside her again. "Just carry on with your plans, Louis. We both know you won't listen to me, what I think, what I feel, what I *want*. It's never enough for you."

"Why is it enough for *you*?"

Her jaw clamped, locking tight, no doubt to keep her from yelling at him. "Don't tell me what I need in my life," she said finally.

He stepped to the piano and casually leaned against it. "You need something?"

"No. And this piano will do. A new one would need tuning after being delivered, anyway." She stood up, shutting the piano cover. "So maybe you should just tune it like you said you would."

Her brown eyes locked on his, challenging him.

"Maybe," he said, taking a step closer, "despite how you try to convince yourself, it's *not* good enough."

"And maybe you don't know everything." She crossed her arms again, her glare set to deep freeze.

He returned it with a wry, understanding smile.

Her expression morphed into something resembling a wounded animal who was lashing out due to pain. The fact that she was feeling this way when she'd been that strong, smart woman he'd known in high school made his heart ache.

"Maybe you should stop accepting things you shouldn't," he said gently.

"The piano's fine, Louis." She seemed strangely calm, as if caught in some weird place between emotions. "Maybe you should accept that not everything needs changing just because you want it to be different."

Fair enough.

But not something he was willing to do.

He moved into her physical space, tempted to cup her chin and kiss her.

"Maybe you need to learn to speak up," he

said. "Demand more. Reach out and grab what you want in life."

"Yeah?" The word came out breathy, not firm like he'd expected. Her eyes flashed with anger—at herself, no doubt, and her tone became hard, flippant. "Then bring me a glorious new piano, Louis, or fulfill your promise to make this thing work again. And while you're at it, how about finding me a job that pays better, too?"

She clamped her mouth shut, catching herself.

Busted. She wasn't satisfied with her job, after all. She wanted more. He rocked back on his heels, reminding himself to play it slow and not go charging in.

She let out a frustrated huff. "Quit trying to mess up my life, Louis. I'm happy! Things are good."

"Follow your dreams, Hannah. Follow the yellow brick road," he crooned.

"Maybe I *am* living my dream."

A single mom working in a job that would never allow her to pay her bills without her ex-husband's support. How could *that* be her dream?

"Maybe there's room for more."

"Like a teaching certificate?" She jutted out a hip, daring him to agree.

He shrugged.

"Going back to school sounds so fun. Let's see..." She ticked things off on her fingers. "I'd be pinched for time, traveling to the city several days a week—if not actually moving there after finally settling the family here, or even worse, leaving the boys behind and becoming a long-distance mom. A busy, distracted, stressed mother, as well as in debt. Sounds like I'll provide my boys the kind of childhood everyone dreams of. And for what? The possibility that I might be able to teach a classroom full of kids and financially support myself and the boys without having to ask Calvin for things like shoes and back-to-school supplies?"

She sucked in a deep breath, her eyes damp.

"Sometimes we have to make minor sacrifices in order to—"

"You're not a parent. You don't understand."

"Enlighten me."

"Try listening!"

"You see the problems, but what about the rewards?" She shut her eyes as he continued. "Financial security. Sharing the same holidays as your sons. Using that amazing brain of yours."

She opened her eyes, a flash of anger reddening her complexion. He softened his tone, reaching for that curl that had sprung loose from her bun. She tipped her head away, her brows scrunched in confusion. He grasped the tendril, stepping closer to delicately tuck it behind her ear. Her throat bobbed as she swallowed nervously. He saw a flash of longing, but didn't know if it was for his touch or for the career and lifestyle he'd described.

"Maybe you need to learn to be happy with what you have," she whispered, her feet tucked between his, their bodies almost touching.

"I'm trying. I keep failing at it."

"Well, maybe I already reached out to get what I want. I have a home. Two kids. A job. A car. I don't need more."

"Did you pick it all out yourself?"

She opened her mouth, then closed it. "Calvin and I decide on many of these things together," she said diplomatically. "As a couple. That's what we do."

Calvin was still running her life, making the major decisions, even in divorce. No wonder she didn't trust herself to make a life-altering choice about going back to school.

"The house?" he asked, curious how deep Calvin was in her life, even though her former marriage was far from being his business.

"It has good insulation. It keeps us cool during the summer."

"What did you pick out?"

"It doesn't matter, Louis. That's the point! He makes good decisions and considers things I don't. Like an all-wheel-drive SUV is better with kids than a cute sedan." She must have caught something in his expression because she stepped back, saying, "I got to veto the expensive bungalow he chose for himself, as well as the bigger SUV he'd thought *I'd* like."

"Okay."

She threw her arms in the air. "So what's your problem?"

"There's no problem."

"Then why are you so bossy?"

"I'm good at it."

"Expert level," she muttered, turning away to sweep a palm through the dust gathered on the piano top, then smacking her hands together to clean them. She gave an adorable sneeze.

"Are you going to look into becoming a teacher?" he asked.

Her tone was exasperated as she marched toward the doors. "Why can't you understand that I'm fine working in a day care?"

"Because you're not."

"Haven't you been listening?"

"I have. Haven't you?"

"To you?"

"No, to yourself."

"What?"

"You're a convincing liar," he said gently.

She gasped with indignation, whirling to face him. "I am *not* lying. To you or myself or anyone else." Her expression turned dark. "I like working there, and I am not being complaisant like you think I am."

He took a steadying breath, considering momentarily if this was the time to stop talking.

"Fine," he said, as she returned to her marching. "But it's not enough."

"It is!"

"Say it 'They don't pay me enough.'"

"Why? Why do you care if my life isn't perfect?"

He caught up with her at the doors, where she had a hand resting above the switches, ready to turn out the lights.

"Don't be afraid to change your life."

Tears welled in her eyes and she blinked them away, then hit the switches, plunging them into darkness. "I'm not afraid of change."

She opened the door and daylight blinded him

from seeing anything other than how she was silhouetted in the doorway—all curvy mom. She was beautiful.

"We just got settled here after a move from the city, separate houses, separate cars, the boys moving between two homes, me in a new job."

"That's a lot of change." He joined her in the doorway.

She cleared her throat. "Cassandra and Athena have things to do, so if you're done pretending you know how to tune a piano, can we go and relieve my babysitters?"

Louis nodded slowly, moving toward his truck, one eye on her.

"You know, not everyone wants to waltz off on adventures, with no cares or responsibilities," she said, her tone a bit preachy as she climbed in the passenger side. "Maybe some of us enjoy having a stable life and don't need more. We don't need to disrupt our lives due to some insatiable thirst for action and excitement. Maybe I just need a job, and a home and movie night with my kids. Maybe that's the important stuff." She fastened her seat belt and locked eyes on Louis. "You know—family."

He could feel Hannah's judgment washing over him, seeping between the cracks. She did have a good life, full of meaning. Who was he to tell her it wasn't important or enough for her?

He looked away. "You're right."

That hollow feeling he usually experienced when he parted ways with Hannah arrived earlier this time, and he focused on starting his truck, driving her home.

"I do know what it's like to have responsibilities," he said quietly, when they turned onto Cherry Lane. "And to have someone depending on you."

Her tone was filled with surprise. "You have kids?"

He gripped the steering wheel, doubting himself. "My mom was sick when I was in high school. I went home at lunch to cook and eat with her before coming back to school again."

"Oh. I didn't know."

That's because they hadn't told many people. It wasn't out of shame or an attempt to dodge pity, but rather his mother's wish for privacy. Even after all these years he still didn't know why he resisted talking about it.

He finally glanced at Hannah. The contemplativeness in her brown eyes made them appear almost black. "You have two amazing sons who seem very well adjusted. That isn't easy."

"It *is* easy." That fight was back and he wondered why he even tried. The woman was exhausting. "Calvin and I get along very well."

Instead of asking what that cost her, he simply said, "I know." He reached out, patting her hand just once while he repeated, "I know."

* * *

The drive back into town had been fast—too fast. And before long they were in front of Hannah's home, where he parked his truck on the street instead of in his driveway. Louis got out with her, eyeing the yard's inflatable Frosty bobbing jovially as the fan at his base kept him plump with air.

He walked Hannah to her door even though he could see from his yard if she got home safely. At the steps she stopped. He'd been hoping she'd invite him in for a second cup of chai with the gals. He liked her friends and the insights they gave him into Hannah.

"Why have you never liked Calvin?" Hannah asked, facing him, her chin tipped up in the weak December sunshine. It was like she had seen into his mind, sorted out the wavelength he had been riding on and then caught that wave herself.

He'd wanted to ask her why she'd married Calvin. Why she'd let him run their lives and then basically leave her behind. Had he ever even loved her the way she deserved?

They were questions he couldn't ask, and her question was one he refused to answer.

He shifted, gazing at the front window of her cabin, at the intricate paper snowflakes she'd no doubt made with the boys. "What does a new piano cost?"

"What?" She blinked a few times. "I'll hire a real tuner. One who has tools and isn't overwhelmed by the number of strings inside."

He smirked. "So, seriously. How much?"

"I asked you a question."

"I asked one, too. How much?"

"A lot."

"How much was yours?" He gestured toward her house and the piano he knew was sitting in the living room.

"A lot."

"You're in a real helpful mood, aren't you?" Her belligerence and the way she was blocking him and his questions made him want to kiss her. Irrational? A bit.

Hannah planted her hands on her hips, so she wouldn't be tempted to swing at him, he figured, or maybe wrap those lovely fingers around his throat and squeeze.

He remained silent and she said, "I wasn't expecting tuning the piano to be such an issue."

"So? It is. Let's solve it. We could restore the old beast, but we don't have a ton of time." Or the skills. "We could replace it."

"The piano actually isn't mine, so I can't just march in there and start solving things." She waved in the direction of the community barn.

"If you plan on playing music for the Christmas concert, then it is your problem."

She shifted her hands on her hips and inhaled slowly. At the sound of a car pulling up she glanced over Louis's shoulder, her lashes fluttering and her bottom lip disappearing between her front teeth.

Louis followed her gaze as she called out, "Man-night Steakfest was yesterday."

Calvin. Pretty nice shiny SUV. Nicer than the vehicle he'd seen Hannah driving.

Calvin came to a halt, staring at the two of them.

Louis grinned, unable to help himself. Calvin was irked to see him, and that made Louis's day. He could be such a petty man when it came to Calvin.

"What do you need?" Hannah asked, her voice lacking the warmth she used to reserve for the man who'd swept her off her feet so many years ago.

Calvin was wearing a fine wool coat and polished black loafers, so he must have come straight from work. Louis wondered how long it would be before he started dating again. Probably not too long. He hoped the self-centered jerk didn't make life miserable for Hannah and the boys when he did.

"I thought we could discuss some last-minute details about Paris," Calvin said, his gaze fixed solidly on Louis.

Paris? What the...?

Louis turned to Hannah, unable to mask his disbelief. "You're going to Paris? With him?"

"Calvin and the boys are going." Hannah gave Louis a look that said "Butt out." Not that he was ever very good at that.

"He's taking the boys?" he asked. How was she not outraged? It was obvious her sons were her life, and Christmas was in eight days. She loved everything about the holiday and surely wanted to pull every joyful morsel out of the lead-up with her kids. More so if they still believed in Santa and the magic of the season.

"Yes." Hannah inhaled slowly, clearly working to keep herself calm.

"Louis Bellmore," Calvin said, his tone flat. "You're back in town."

Louis stood taller. "Living right next door."

His smile sure felt smug. He hoped it looked it, too.

Calvin took a long look at Hannah, then shifted his attention back to Louis. His jaw was tight, like the time Louis had spotted him in the grocery store with his sons and they were begging for him to buy a carton of grape juice.

"Of course you are," Calvin said tightly.

"Indeed I am." Louis grinned and rocked back on his heels. "And you're still...you?"

Hannah flashed him a warning look, having noted the hint of insult in his words and tone. Couldn't get much past her. That was one of the things he admired most about her.

"Thomas has a play date and the ladies are over," Hannah said, moving toward the steps again.

"Then what are you two doing out here?" Calvin asked.

He'd come closer to Hannah, his eyes still on Louis, staking his territory, no doubt. He might not want her any longer, but he sure didn't want

Louis anywhere near her. The jerk was smart enough to know he hadn't done well by Hannah and that Louis would call him on it. Or do better, if given the chance.

"Talking." Hannah crossed her arms, then softened her stance when Calvin gave her a wounded look. "We were checking out the piano for the concert."

"Hannah believes it's had its season," Louis said. He eyed Calvin's Buick. It was freshly washed, all glossy and perfect. Not a speck of Texas dust had dared settle on it yet. "I was thinking I'd scour the used ads, but maybe you'd care to donate one? Your wife sure could use it to accompany the kids at the Christmas concert."

Hannah gave Louis a warning look while Calvin crossed his arms, his chest puffed out.

"He can't afford another piano," Hannah muttered. Louder, she added, "I need to check in with the gals."

She'd turned, about to climb the steps, when Louis muttered, "Spent it all on the Buick, huh?"

She glowered at him in a way that no doubt worked on her boys when they misbehaved.

"You need a piano, honey?" Calvin cozied up to Hannah, sliding an arm around her shoulders. He bumped his hip against hers, and Louis could see the way she softened before catching herself. She pushed him off her, giving him a glare she normally reserved for Louis when she was itching for a gun.

"Why didn't you say something?" Calvin asked her. "I bet the engineering company I work for would be more than happy to donate one. And if not, maybe I can find one like I did for your living room."

"You'll find one?" She turned, her face lighting up, and Louis cursed himself for the way he'd set Calvin up to be the hero. Her expression grew wary. "You leave for France tomorrow. I'm going to need the piano right after you get back, and it'll have to be tuned after being delivered."

"I can tune it," Louis interjected.

"By a professional," she added, not even glancing his way.

Calvin let out a huff of amusement, his features relaxing. "You two still hate each other, huh?"

"We don't hate each other," Hannah snapped.

"Hey! Look who's here," Athena called from the doorway. "I thought I heard voices. How's the piano?"

Obi scampered down the steps to circle the men before sitting at Hannah's feet. He stretched his neck and nudged Louis's hand, hoping for some attention, which Louis provided with a scratch behind the ears.

Calvin whistled for the dog, but Obi, now in ear-rubbing ecstasy, ignored him.

"The piano's fine," Hannah told Athena.

"Hannah won't say it, but it could really use replacing," Louis interjected. He locked his gaze on hers. "She's too forgiving. She could do a lot better than settle."

Hannah narrowed her eyes, and Louis guessed that rage was slowly building inside her, like lava in an active volcano. He really needed to stop pushing her buttons. One of these days he was going to be the victim of vehicular manslaughter or die of poisoned chocolate-cherry cookies.

"But don't worry," he added brightly. "Wonder boy here says he'll get her one." He jerked a thumb in Calvin's direction.

"Really?" Athena's forehead furrowed.

"I'll look into getting something brought in," Calvin said smoothly.

"Aren't you leaving, like, tomorrow?" Athena asked.

"I've got this," he assured her.

"I'm going to go next door," Louis said, feeling like his work had been done and it was time to give it space to play out. He softly tapped Hannah's shoulder. "Open your window and holler if you need anything." He winked at her while giving Obi-Wan an extra goodbye scratch.

Hannah rolled onto the balls of her feet. She almost looked as though she didn't want him to leave.

"She won't need you," Calvin said tightly, his hands curling into fists. "She has me."

"In...Frankfurt, was it?"

"France."

"Ah. Right." He nodded, letting Calvin stew over the fact that while he was away, Louis was going to be living right next door to his ex.

* * *

"It doesn't make sense," Hannah complained to Cassandra, ten minutes after Louis had left, followed by Calvin and Athena.

"It makes total sense," her friend replied, palms flat on the kitchen table. "Calvin's jealous of Louis and vice versa."

"It still doesn't make sense."

"Louis has a thing for you, which is driving Calvin nuts."

"But Calvin doesn't want me." Never mind the

erroneous fact that Louis wanted her. He wanted to irk, rile, pester and bother her. Nothing romantic.

"Just because Calvin is moving on doesn't mean he wants his old rival to win you. And why else would Louis pretend he can tune a piano except for the fact that he likes you?" Cassandra laughed. She'd loved hearing the story of Louis's moxie, going all the way to the barn and never quite admitting he was in over his head.

"He would do all of that to annoy me," Hannah replied.

"It's only annoying because you like him, but don't want to." She smiled as if she'd hit upon some truth—which she hadn't.

Louis and Hannah? They were like ketchup on pudding. It just didn't work.

"He's annoying. He's still pushy. And thinks he knows what's best for me. He intentionally made Calvin jump in and say he'd secure a new piano."

"Smart man." Cassandra was grinning.

"Louis shouldn't have done that to Calvin." He'd played to her ex's insecurities and weaknesses.

She could see how easy it had been, but still.

And why hadn't Louis stepped up with his big NHL coaching salary and bought a new piano if he was so intent on puffing out his chest?

Secretly, Hannah hoped Calvin would solve the community's piano problem if for no other reason than to have Louis's plan blow up in his face.

"And before you guilt-talk yourself too much about the piano, the one at the barn *is* old," Cass said. "And it's not like Calvin's broke. Louis probably did you and the community a favor." She moved toward the front door, hollering for Dusty, who had finished helping Thomas tidy up the toys they'd been playing with. They were now in that precious, momentary balance where it was imperative to extract the boys before the mess was recreated.

"And," she added, reaching for the door even though her son was still in Thomas's room, and by the sounds of it, trying to see who could launch LEGO pieces the farthest, "I also happen to agree with Louis that you should become a teacher."

Hannah gave her a skeptical look.

"It'll only take a few courses, right?"

Hannah folded her arms across her chest. It was more than "just a few."

Cass lowered her voice. "Thomas really likes him and so does Obi."

"So?"

Cassandra raised her brows, calling Hannah on her feigned obtuseness. It was impossible to overlook the way Louis was hitting some pretty important marks on a single mom's potential-new-husband list. Good with your kid? Check. The dog likes him? Another check. He had earned himself a free pass straight to the inner circle, where his eligibility could be considered more fully. Because chances were that having earned those two checkmarks meant he was a good person.

Annoying, but good. Handsome, too.

"He likes a life full of adventure," Hannah said. "He's not looking to play daddy."

Cassandra smirked, and Hannah paused, wondering why her excuse felt like a lie. Did he actually want a family? She almost felt as though he might. If she was a decent judge of character—and she liked to think that she was—it seemed as though he might actually *want* a cozy family life.

Hannah shook her head. She was projecting her own desires onto him. He was a pilot, a guy who'd had a million careers already and was currently coaching a professional hockey team over an hour away. He wasn't about to spend an evening at home watching movies with her and the boys. Settling down and being part of a family wasn't his lifestyle.

Cassandra hollered for Dusty again. "Come on, kid! Levi Wylder's waiting for us to pick up that saddle blanket for Auntie Alexa. We need to get moving. Chop, chop!" She lowered her voice. "As for Louis, why don't you kiss him and see if all this fighting is just chemistry with nowhere to go?"

Hannah gave a huff of amusement as Dusty surfaced from Thomas's room, Wade appearing momentarily to wave goodbye. Cassandra plunked a red knitted hat on Dusty's curls as he slipped on his boots. She had him out the door in seconds, adding, "Be like Nike, my friend. Just do it."

Hannah waved goodbye and closed the door to find Wade already in front of the TV.

"Did I say yes to screen time?"

"Yup."

"I didn't. Turn it off."

"But I'm tired and wanna watch."

"Why don't you and Thomas finish your letters to Santa so I can mail them? That way they'll get to him in time for Christmas."

Wade rolled his eyes, but kept his mouth shut about the existence of Santa Claus as Thomas tore into the kitchen, yelling, "Santa!" He yanked his half-written letter from the fridge, sending the magnet flying. As nice as the upcoming break would be while they were in France, she was going to miss her little whirlwind.

Just pretend he's going to be over at Calvin's for a week and not half a world away.

Hannah sighed and held up the list of things to pack for Wade and Thomas that Calvin had left with her. It was long, but she could see at a glance it was missing important items, such as Thomas's favorite teddy bear and Wade's allergy medication. She tossed the list aside, wondering what Calvin would do if she ignored it.

Right. He'd be steamed up, because it was Hannah who took care of the details, desperately hanging on to her sons and the idea of being needed.

What had changed, that she no longer relished the idea of being involved with the trip, even if it was just to help with packing? Was it her secret snarky side—usually reserved for Louis—rearing up and expanding into all areas of her life? Did she believe that if Calvin was going to take their sons on an international trip, then he should be in charge from start to finish? That he was on his own and could very well mess up and fail? Did she want the vacation to be miserable for her boys? For Calvin to be trekking out into the night to buy allergy tablets? Because that's what could happen if she didn't add items to his list.

"How do you spell 'Mercedes'?" Thomas asked.

"You don't need a car," she replied absently, picking up Calvin's list again.

"Dad wants it."

"He already has a nice car."

Because he made more money than a day care worker did. Because he'd taken care of himself by getting a degree, instead of quitting like she had, floating along, assuming he'd always be there. And now he wasn't.

She plunked herself down at the table and shoved her hands in her hair. She was a grown-up and couldn't afford the same things her former partner could, even though they'd been hip to hip all their adult lives.

Maybe going back to school would be smart, even if challenging for her and the family.

Her phone beeped with a text from Calvin, saying there were no used pianos online in the area, and that maybe the concert's organizing group could sort something out in time.

Hannah put her phone down, wanting to ghost him by not replying. Instead, she picked it up again and sent him a thumbs-up emoji, hating the way she was letting him off the hook, but very aware that she was preventing a fight, which was probably what Louis had been angling to create.

Hannah shifted her chair closer to Thomas's, clutching her phone as she reminded him to put spaces between his words so Santa could read the letter easier. She wondered what Louis had asked Santa for at this age.

And how had nobody known that his mother was sick while he was in high school? How had his family managed to keep that private in a town like Sweetheart Creek? And why did that tidbit of his history feel connected to the way he'd judged her and her life choices back then?

Had Hannah messed up in her assessment of Louis somewhere along the line? But then why had he judged her so harshly for wanting to start a family with Calvin, when today his eyes had softened when talking about kids?

Again, she was getting the puzzle instead of the toy in the chocolate egg surprise that was Louis Bellmore.

4

Hannah kept waving even after her former father-in-law turned the corner, driving Wade, Thomas and Calvin to the airport along with Calvin's mom. Finally, Hannah lowered her arm, letting her shoulders sag. She swiped at her eyes with her middle fingers, frustrated that her plan of wearing non-waterproof mascara hadn't worked to keep the tears at bay. She was going to end up looking like a racoon with her smeared makeup.

Obi nudged her thigh with his nose as she sniffed back the tears.

"I know," she said, her voice wobbling. The temptation to shove items into a suitcase and follow her kids to the airport was far too great.

She inhaled deeply. She no longer belonged with Calvin, and they were no longer a family unit. Calvin's mother was going on the reconnaissance trip to act as chief caregiver for the boys while Calvin was in meetings. As Cassandra had said, Calvin and the boys wouldn't always be front and center in Hannah's life, and in this moment the fact had never felt so true.

She needed to stand on her own two feet, starting right now. She stared at her house, the urge to make an instant move down the path of significant life changes itching like mad. She still hadn't heard back from Athena about admissions into the education program, and until she knew more about going back to school she didn't want to tease herself with dreams of a career change. Maybe she could do something less extreme and finally paint Wade's bedroom. He hated the beige color the former owners had chosen, and he wanted blue.

Forcing her feet to move, Hannah headed back to the warm house. Inside, she kicked off her shoes and stared at the black TV screen in the living room.

Tonight was movie night. She and Calvin had a deal around movie night and Steakfest. She got movie night even on his week to have the boys, and he got what he, his dad and the boys called Steakfest, where the four of them went out for steak and acted like cavemen. Well, maybe not cavemen exactly, but whatever it was, Calvin's dad promised it would put hair on the boys' chests, something they were quite enthused about.

Hannah dropped heavily onto the couch. She hadn't missed a movie night with her sons since they'd moved in, a year ago.

No. No feeling sorry for herself. This was an opportunity for all of them. The boys would gain some independence while seeing more of the world, and she would watch something rated higher than PG tonight. Hannah could curl up in bed with a glass of wine and a movie, or she could eat junk food on the couch. She could even turn the music up too loud. No rules. No mommying.

She nodded to herself, feeling bolstered. But then began to shake her head. The house was too quiet. Too...dull and lifeless. She got up and plugged in the Christmas tree. Pretty. She waited for the spirit of the holidays to envelop her with its warmth and cheer. Instead, the cold reality of loneliness crept in.

This was exactly what Cassandra had been warning her about.

Outside. She needed to go outside.

Hannah hustled to the door and pulled on her jacket, stuffing a thin pair of gloves in her pocket. A brisk morning walk would clear her mind and help her find much-needed Zen head space.

"Walkies!" she called to Obi, and he came scurrying around the corner, his nails clacking on the floor.

Hannah clipped the leash to his collar and in moments they were out in the sunshine as it crested the oaks that encircled the town of Sweetheart Creek. The morning rays set the town aglow with a magical, ethereal feeling. She hurried down the steps and headed south, hanging a left at the high school, then continued out of town, where the road turned to gravel. Hannah released Obi from his leash as they passed Violet Granger's place, which was an old B and B called Peach Blossom Hollow. After that the road narrowed, weaving past Old Man Lovely's chapel on the hill, and soon Hannah was trailing after Obi along a grassy path that skirted the edge of the creek, heading toward the swimming hole.

Twenty minutes later, huffing and puffing, Hannah took the worn wooden steps up the slope to the slow moving water that spilled into the pool. She stopped short in front of a tall metal gate ladened with small locks, ribbons and charms that glittered in the morning sun. She'd forgotten about Lock Gate, and how it had once been part of a large fence to keep kids out of the swimming hole. In the 1980s a teen had drowned during a late-night party there, and the community had barricaded the area. Originally, padlocks had been fastened to the gate along with a ribbon and a prayer for the young man who'd drowned. Over the years the rest of the fence had fallen or been knocked down, reopening the swimming hole. The gate, however, had remained, now heavy with locks, wishes and prayers that extended well beyond the fallen teenager who had started it all.

When Hannah was a teen, folks had said that fastening two locks together on the gate meant their owners would become lovers for life. So Calvin and she had taken the combination locks from their lockers out to the gate on the last day of high school. But when Calvin had opened his backpack, his padlock was gone.

Coincidence? Bad luck? Foreshadowing? She didn't want to consider what might have happened if they'd managed to hang their locks together.

Gazing at the gate now, Hannah shook her head. How innocent and full of hope she'd been.

As she continued down to the shore, skirting the rapids, she spotted someone on the path ahead. Hannah called out an apology when Obi went bounding over, and the figure turned. Louis. Her heart gave a little skip, but she wasn't sure if it was due to anticipation or dread.

"Hey, Hannah."

"Hey."

"You saw your little men off okay?"

She bit the inside of her cheek, trying to trap the sudden welling of emotion so she wouldn't start blubbering like a fool. She gave a short nod.

France was so far away and the three of them had never been so far apart, or for so long.

Wordlessly, Louis came over and rested a hand on her shoulder. The unexpected empathy made her eyes fill with tears. She was still wearing that crappy mascara and she shifted away, desperate to regain control.

"I guess it'll give you some peace and quiet so you can apply for college, huh?" There was a twinkle of amusement in Louis's eyes and she retaliated, giving him a playful shove.

"You're a brat."

His feet slipped on the loose stones at the edge of the creek and, horrified, she reached out to catch him before he fell into the cold water. Her hands slid around his waist so she was pressed to him as he continued to wobble. His arms clenched tight around her as they struggled for balance.

Then just as suddenly as he'd tipped and slipped, he righted himself with a chuckle, causing her to realize he'd never been in real danger of falling.

"Seriously?" Hannah angled her head up to glare at him as she dropped her arms. He kept his locked around her as Obi danced about, barking happily.

"It's been some time since a beautiful woman wrapped her arms around me." Louis was giving her a lovely, comforting hug, his black Dragons jacket warm from the sun. She loved it. She hated it.

She pushed him away, wriggling from his grip.

"What are you doing out here?" She felt as though she'd given up something by letting him hug her for so long. "Adding a lock to the gate with your invisible girlfriend?"

"Something like that."

Hannah watched him for a moment, his gold-flecked blue eyes studying hers.

"What?" he asked, that crooked smile fading.

She shrugged, suddenly unsure. He'd looked as though he was going to say something else, then changed his mind.

"What?" she echoed. This was becoming awkward fast. And since things with Louis never got awkward, this was new ground, and she didn't particularly like it.

"Want to walk with me?" he asked, the awkwardness dissolving as quickly as it had appeared. He held out his hand, offering assistance down a particularly slick, muddy part of the trail. It was sheltered by the large oak trees surrounding the swimming hole and creek, and was frequently splashed with water.

"Okay." She let her gloved hand slide into his, tempted to fake slipping to see if he'd catch her.

How mixed up was her head if his hug seemed like the best part of her day?

They carried on down the slope, Louis dropping her hand where the trail narrowed between some bushes, this route less traveled as they headed away from the pond. Obi-Wan loped ahead of them, his fringed tail making happy circles in the air.

"Louis?" Hannah ventured.

"Yeah?" He looked at her over his shoulder

and she was hit by the directness of his gaze. He was so handsome, and so kind when he wanted to be. And he took the crap she blasted at him.

Unable to summon the courage to say what was on her mind, she replied, "Nothing."

"What?"

"It'll sound bad," she admitted.

"I don't mind bad."

"I know." It was one of the reasons she liked him—very much against her will, of course. "I just wanted to say thanks."

"For what?" He turned again, his steps slowing.

"For letting me knock you around with my words."

He stopped so suddenly she almost walked into the team logo stitched onto the back of his jacket. She halted, standing too close, then stumbled back a step. Louis's brow was deeply furrowed, as if she'd just told him she was with the space agency and the world was in danger of being hit by a meteor.

"You don't knock me around."

"I know. You're tough. But sometimes I come close, and I hope you know it's not personal—not really. It never has been."

"Okay."

"It's just that when I'm with you I..." She floundered, unable to explain what she called the Louis Effect. So often when she was with him every frustration and shortcoming came to the surface, in need of release, and so she blasted it all at him like toxic waste.

He freed her to be bold, fully honest with nothing held back. But that came with a cost. She might be free to explore her thoughts and feelings without worrying about reining herself in, but it often meant she didn't treat him kindly. And she didn't like that. She didn't like how badly she reacted, or how she felt like such a poor excuse for a human after her temper had cooled and her common sense returned.

She tried again. "When I'm with you, I'm..."

"When you're with me, you're you," he said simply, breaking into a wide, warm smile.

"But I'm mean. I don't want to be mean."

"Then don't be."

"It just happens."

"You haven't hurt me. I'm okay." He was watching her steadily. "I know who you are. I can see beyond that."

She stared at him for a long moment, hoping he was telling her the truth. Because, in a lot of ways, she was her genuine self around him and was able to speak about how she felt—even if those truths might be ugly or unpopular, fueled by her insecurities and fears.

Finally, she nodded, wishing he'd hug her again.

They walked in silence until they reached the outskirts of town.

"Louis?"

"Yeah?"

Hannah sucked in a deep breath, then asked the scariest question she could think of. "Do you want to be my friend?"

* * *

Friend?

This was real life, right? He wasn't having some twisted stress dream where she said this and then pushed him off a cliff or something, was he?

"Sure," Louis said, as they continued walking toward Cherry Lane.

Friend.

They stopped on the sidewalk in front of their houses, shifting their weight, unsure what to say.

It was easier being enemies.

Hannah released Obi, who shot off into the backyard.

"Thanks for letting me walk with you," Louis said, filling the silence.

Hannah hesitated. "Is your mom…" She looked down, then asked, "Where are you spending Christmas? Do you exchange gifts? Do you still despise Christmas?" Catching herself, she added, "Sorry, it's none of my business."

"I thought we were *friends*."

"I know, but..." She was smiling. That beautiful one that was a mix of bashful curiosity and happiness. It was an unstoppable smile, and usually reserved for Calvin and friends. Had Louis truly made the cut? The idea made him want to freeze this moment.

"Is my mom still alive?" he asked carefully, starting with her first question. "Unfortunately, she passed away."

"I'm so sorry."

He reached out, tapped the back of her gloved hand. "My life can be your business, Hannah."

"Sorry, I just—I don't want to overstep. It feels like this could be a no-go area."

He stepped a little closer, peering at her. "It's not. I'm an open book."

She didn't reply, and he said, "Ask me anything. Feel free. But first, to quickly answer your previous questions, I'm spending Christmas with my dad and I still don't go nuts over the holiday like some people."

She narrowed her eyes. "I don't go nuts."

"Sure."

"I don't."

"Okay."

There was something in her steady, assessing gaze that made him cringe. It was as though she was preparing herself to analyze the truth of his response to a question she hadn't yet asked.

"Do you really know how to tune a piano?"

Louis tipped his head back and laughed. He'd forgotten just how direct she could be.

He met her eyes, loving the way her mouth was twisted with mischief. "I've had the best online video teacher there is," he admitted.

"I do admire your confidence. I hope my boys grow up to be…"

Louis felt his breath stick in his chest. "Would it be so bad if they turned out like me?"

"I don't particularly want to fight with them all the time."

"So? Then don't fight with me." He angled closer, his feet bracketing hers. Her breathing slowed as she stared up at him.

His next move felt like it might be a kiss.

He knew it was way too early for that. It would be like dropping a bomb when negotiations had only just begun.

He brushed back a strand of hair that wasn't tucked under her hat.

"But that's what we do," she said, her voice breathy. "We fight."

"It's not a rule."

"It isn't?"

"No." He kept his voice low, confiding. His lips had somehow moved closer to hers, and he waited, curious about how she'd react. The warmth from their breath battled the chilly morning air surrounding them. "And we don't fight. It's more like we challenge each other."

She met his steady gaze, not backing out of his personal space, but looking at him with defiance, as if facing down an inner demon.

"I think we're going to make great friends," he said. He brushed the sides of her arms, his mouth still angled like it might land on hers sometime soon. She was leaning in.

But then her nerves got the best of her and she laughed.

"You don't want to be my friend?" He leaned away, giving her some space.

"No, that's not it," she said quickly. "I want to be friends, but we...we had a love-hate relationship in high school," she stated, her expression apologetic, slightly panicked. "But without the love part. Can we actually hang out and not kill each other?" Her laugh was awkward. "Because this *thing* that's happening—" she pointed to the narrow space between them "—is feeling like we're missing a pretty big step, and you should know that I'm done with love and relationships and everything else."

So she had felt it, too.

That was good.

Even if she was telling him there was no chance she'd ever consider a relationship that went beyond friends.

She swallowed hard. She wouldn't look at him, and he had a feeling she'd wanted to get swept up in the moment despite her reservations.

Did she worry that he'd tire of her, leave her high and dry like Calvin had? Or was she worried he wasn't serious about things like relationships and would break her heart?

And possibly her boys' hearts, too.

Louis gently cupped Hannah's face and she flinched, but when he didn't advance, didn't move or speak, she finally looked up, her long lashes creating shadows over the smudges of mascara under her tired brown eyes.

"Take a breath," he instructed. He inhaled slowly to demonstrate.

"I am!" She wasn't. She was freaking out.

"Learn this, okay? Love alone isn't enough to bring happiness," he said. "You need more than that. We all do. And yes, I would have loved to kiss you a moment ago. You didn't imagine it."

Her mouth dropped open, then clamped shut again. He quickly placed a finger over her lips before she could say anything. "But even more than that, I would love to be your friend. It's okay if you're not looking to jump into something right now, and I respect and honor that."

The fight went out of her, and her shoulders softened. He pulled her into his arms, hugging her.

"I'm sorry that your love for Calvin wasn't returned in the way you wanted. Everyone deserves to be loved back, with just as much oomph as they feel."

He paused when a hiccupy sound escaped, and released her when she raised her hands between them, wiping up tears that had pooled between her lashes.

Louis pulled a clean tissue from his coat pocket and dried her cheeks.

It felt like he'd brought her to tears a couple of times today. He had to leave for practice soon, but maybe tonight, when he was home again, he could do something for her. Help build her back up so she could be the superwoman she needed to be when her boys returned.

"Where was that tissue when Thomas had his nosebleed?" she muttered.

Louis chuckled. "I decided it would be smart to keep a couple stashed in my pocket. I do have a rather active seven-year-old living next door. And his mom, as you may have heard, could use a little help when he gets nosebleeds."

He gently wiped away the last tear and Hannah leaned into him. "Thank you," she whispered.

"You're welcome." He wadded the damp tissue into a ball, holding back from pulling her against him again. "What are you up to next?"

"It's movie night tonight," she said, with a quaver in her voice.

He captured her face in his hands, tipped it down and placed a kiss on top of her hat, then took a few steps backward. "Thanks for the walk, Hannah."

And he strode away, wishing it was easy. Wishing he could pull her under his wing, kiss her on the lips and be everything she needed in order to be strong.

* * *

Hannah watched Louis walk into his house before she went into her own, feeling oddly rejected. Somehow he'd broken her open, making her feel both vulnerable and connected, and then he'd just turned and left.

How had she considered for even one second that Louis Bellmore could be the man she needed? He wasn't equipped to handle weepy women or lonely moms, and currently, she was both.

Hannah threw her jacket, hat, and gloves across the room in frustration. Obi chased down the striped hat, retrieving it with enthusiasm. Rubbing his ears, she sighed and told him he was a good dog, then took the slobbery hat and tossed it into the wicker basket under the bench at the door.

Why had she exposed herself to Louis like that? And why had she taken their almost-kiss and made it into a big deal, telling him she didn't want a relationship?

It was true, because something like that would only complicate everything at the moment, but had she really needed to turn a pleasant walk into a grand shutdown?

But he'd said he wanted to kiss her which made no sense. She couldn't possibly be his type, and she couldn't figure out why he'd want to be with her. He'd be bored in five minutes.

Hannah leaned against the door and touched her lips, curious how it would feel to kiss him. Would he be tender? Or would kissing him bring on the crazy sparks she'd read about in romance novels?

She groaned in frustration and faced the empty house. Now what? She couldn't start watching movies before noon. Not that she really wanted to. Maybe she could pretend today wasn't movie night, or that it didn't exist when the boys were away.

Hannah didn't have any piano lessons to prep for until January, but she had presents she could wrap as a distraction. She could also get lost in the memoir Athena had brought her.

But instead of heading to her bookcase or digging out the wrapping paper, Hannah sat down at her old laptop, waiting while it whirled and hummed, struggling to boot up and get online.

If she was heading back to school she'd need a computer upgrade. Plus teachers were expected to do some work from home, and so much of it was computer-based these days.

What was she thinking? She wasn't going to become a teacher.

Instead of going to the college website like she'd planned, Hannah closed the laptop and leaned back in her chair, mulling over her feelings. She checked her phone for messages and saw a text from Athena. Her friend in admissions had said that, as a mature student, if Hannah applied before his holidays started on Tuesday, she'd know before January if she'd been accepted and whether they could fit her into the program. As well, he'd mentioned that the first four classes toward her degree could be taken online, and that she might qualify for scholarships.

Could it really be that easy? Just apply, get in and win a few scholarships to cover her costs?

Hannah set her phone down and moved to the piano, breathing in the familiar smell of freshly applied polish. She lifted the lid and ran her fingers lightly over the keys. This old friend could get her through any funk, and she was certain that once she finished playing she'd have the answer on what to do about Louis and school.

As her fingers struck the first chords of "O Come All Ye Faithful" her mind snapped out of thinking mode. She became one with the music, the energy and peacefulness of the carol flowing through her.

She swayed, becoming her own metronome to keep the beat. Everything that wasn't about this moment could wait for another day, another time. Song after song, she played through the afternoon, until the early dusk of Texas Hill Country settled in around her. The muscles between her shoulders had grown tight and she rounded her back, stretching them out. She was ravenous, but her mind was finally blessedly blank.

Hannah ran her fingers noiselessly over the keys in a silent thank-you before closing the lid, then stayed there for several more moments.

She was lonely.

Not fully satisfied with where her life path had taken her.

She blinked at her surroundings, at the family photos lining the end tables and fireplace mantel. The Christmas tree and the decorations brightening the room. There was so much to be grateful for, but it no longer felt like enough.

She'd led herself into a corner, her future not quite as open and full of opportunity as she'd once expected it to be. Calvin was treating the boys to a trip to France, a day at Disneyland Paris, a week of eating out and staying in hotels, and she was at home counting her pennies. She'd gone wrong somewhere, hadn't she?

Before she could change her mind, she opened her laptop and filled out the application to enroll in college. Several minutes later she hit Submit and sat back, hands shaking.

She'd done it. She'd applied to go back to school.

She didn't have to say yes if they accepted her, but she'd opened a door to see what might come through it.

The doorbell rang, sending Obi into a flurry of barking, and making her jump. She shut down the computer and peered through the peephole before opening the front door to what would surely become an unexpected adventure.

* * *

"I ate the last cookie," Louis announced, stepping past Hannah, a shopping bag nestled in his arms.

"I know. You already brought back my container."

"Hey, pup." He bent to ruffle the long fur on Obi's back, making the dog grin. He straightened and tipped his shopping bag Hannah's way so she could peek inside at the popcorn, candy and drinks he'd brought. "I thought maybe you could use some company for movie night."

Hannah gave him a radiant smile and threw her arms around him, the bag crinkling as it was crushed against him. He smelled like fresh air, and his jacket released a chill from its folds, reminding her he'd been in an arena all afternoon.

"I think I'm going to like movie night," he said, wrapping his free arm around her waist. "What else happens? Any kissing?" He waggled his eyebrows as she stepped out of his embrace, laughing despite how, only hours earlier, she'd called them out about almost kissing.

Was it possible that he could make her less-than-fun moments laughable? He wanted to be the man who, when she thought her whole world was about to fall apart or get complicated, could simply walk through the door and make everything feel better.

Right now, the tense lines that had framed her mouth before he'd flown out to coach hockey practice were gone. But she had an odd expression in her eyes, as if she was puzzled.

"What?" he asked. "You have a funny look on your face."

"I'm thinking."

"You're not thinking about kissing, though," he mused. "Your expression isn't dreamy enough."

"I keep catching myself liking you."

"Well, you should like your *friends*. And shouldn't that be a dreamy look if you *like* me?"

"How's this?" She clamped her hands together under her chin and batted her lashes.

Sassy. Just the way he loved her.

"Remind me again why I agreed to be friends?" he asked as he kicked off his shoes.

"You're funny, Louis. Cocky, but funny. And you need someone to keep you in line. I'm that gal."

"I prefer the term *confident* over cocky."

He handed her the snack bag and she nosed through the contents. "What's the tablet for?" she asked, lifting it out.

"I have some movies on it. You probably have something lined up already, though?"

"Are you trying to curb your bossiness?"

"How am I doing?"

"Not bad. Even though you did invite yourself over."

He caught Hannah's smile and he gave a small shake of his head before leading her to the kitchen, taking the bag back from her so he could make the microwave popcorn while she opened the iced tea.

When they were ready, they settled on the living room couch, the best seat in the house.

"So? What are we watching?" he asked. He caught sight of a framed photo on the side table and tipped it toward him to take a better look. Hannah and the boys mugging for the camera. He let out a chuckle and set it back again.

"Well," she said slowly, "I usually choose a romantic comedy, and then the boys and I have a discussion afterward about respecting our partners and how communication is the key to any successful relationship."

Louis tossed popcorn at her.

"Hey!"

"You're a liar. I bet you watch animated kids' movies each and every time."

She smirked, and he chucked another piece of popcorn at her. In a flash, she opened her mouth and leaned to the side, catching it with a satisfying crunch. “Thank you.”

Man, she was sexy. With her mussed-up hair, sassy attitude and the way she rolled with the punches. Yet she wasn’t made of Teflon, and he knew that beneath the veneer was a vulnerable woman he needed to cherish and protect.

He opened a bag of chocolate-covered raisins and chucked one her way, but it bounced off her teeth. Hannah scrambled after it just as Obi lunged, his efforts hampered by the slippery hardwood flooring. “Raisins are bad for dogs. So is chocolate.” She grabbed it just in time.

“Sorry. You get it?” Louis asked, leaning forward to snag Obi’s collar.

“Yep.” Hannah popped the raisin in her mouth. “Five-second rule. Did you say something about supper?”

“Bachelor supper. Popcorn.” He turned the screen of his tablet so Hannah could see the title of a romantic comedy. “How about this one?”

“Are you sure you’re up for a discussion about relationships and gender roles?” she teased.

“Maybe we could skip deciphering all that and just enjoy it. Or make out.”

He laughed at her expression. She should be put off by his jokes about kissing, but her cheeks grew pink every time and made it much too tempting to stop. Besides, he figured she might be disappointed if he did let up.

"I've wanted to see that one for a long time," Hannah admitted.

"I hear there could be some scary parts, like a breakup," he said seriously. He slung his right arm across the back of the couch and tipped his chin toward the space beside him. "If you need to move over this way, I'll protect you."

"You're funny."

"Not cocky?"

"Not always. Just ninety-nine percent of the time."

From his side of the couch he heard Hannah's stomach rumble.

"Interested in pizza?" he asked.

"I'm on a budget." She held up a hand. "Don't say it."

"Say what?"

"That I should fight for more hours at the day care, even though the other mom..." Hannah shook her head, as if her argument didn't matter, that he wouldn't listen to it. Which was true. In Louis's mind she was equally deserving, and nothing else mattered. She needed to stop giving up something as vital as her financial independence.

He scooted closer.

"Hey," he said softly. Hannah faced him, arms crossed, ready for a lecture. "I like that you're kind, generous, and think of others. Those are good qualities, you know."

Blinking, Hannah stared at him. "And...?"

He felt like she was waiting for him to call her complaisant—putting the needs and wishes of others before herself. Studying her, he could see that she already felt ashamed for not standing up for herself financially, and that his pushing might cause her to feel worse about herself rather than motivate her to do more.

"And what?" he asked gently.

"We're long overdue for an argument, so go ahead and say it."

He sighed.

"Come on, we've spent several fight-free hours together and I know what you're thinking," she said.

He scooted even closer, his arm still slung over the back of the cushions. He was near enough that he could feel the heat from her leg, her torso. He slowly brushed a thumb down her cheek. "Even though I don't always understand you, I think you're pretty special."

"And?"

"And that's all."

She stared at him for a long moment, as though watching for a tell that would show her he was lying. A flicker in his eyelids, a fidgeting hand.

But he wasn't lying.

"That's all?" she whispered.

"Well, one more thing."

She sat straighter.

"I would still like to kiss you," he stated, his thumb caressing her cheek, "though I'm pretty sure you'll say no."

* * *

Hannah stared at Louis, processing his words. He thought she was special. And he didn't appear to be lying, not that lying was his style.

And he wanted to kiss her.

She shifted closer, trying not to question what she was doing as she allowed her lips to gently land against his.

His kiss was careful, as though he was afraid to take too much. It was gentle, and she sighed against him, folding herself into his arms to lengthen the contact.

He was a good kisser and she studiously refrained from thinking why. In this moment he was hers. Only hers.

"I think I do like movie night," he murmured when they broke apart, her body still comfortably nestled in his embrace.

"And I think I like being friends." She couldn't stop grinning.

"Actually, I don't think that's a good idea," he said solemnly.

Her heart dropped. "Why not?"

Smiling, he lifted her chin and gave her a short, sweet kiss. "Friends don't usually do this."

"Mmm." That was true.

He kissed her again.

"That is problematic," she whispered. "Because I was intrigued by the idea of being your friend."

He tightened his grip, holding her close like there was no way they were going back to just-friends or pretending these kisses didn't happen.

It was a terrifying idea that they'd stepped over a line, taking a one-way street with no chance of doubling back to where they'd started.

But maybe that wasn't such a problem, because kissing him felt right. It felt like something she could do for the rest of her life and not tire of it.

It certainly didn't hurt that he was tall, dark and handsome, with hair long enough to grip with her fingers. She hadn't known she had a thing for men who looked like Dakota warriors, but she certainly did. Especially with that steadying gaze he was giving her, so grounded and present in the moment. It made her insides bubble, and that was scary.

"You know that whatever we're doing together—" Hannah gave a vague wave of her hand "—doesn't mean I'm going to back down."

"What are you saying?" He sat a little straighter.

They needed rules if they were crossing lines.

"Just because we kissed," she clarified, "doesn't mean I'm not going to fight with you, or not dish it back when you deserve it."

He relaxed against the back of the couch. "I'm counting on it, Hannah-Banana." He tucked her against him again before hitting the button to start the movie, ignoring the way she'd growled at the silly nickname. He pressed a kiss to her earlobe as an apology and she shivered.

She didn't know whether to focus on the opening scenes of the movie or the fact that Louis had kissed her and nobody had been murdered. In fact, she'd liked it. A lot.

Hannah's stomach rumbled loudly again and she mentally ran through her December budget. Highest heating bill of the year. Presents. Her plans to paint Wade's bedroom. The college application fee. There was no way she could squeeze in eating out. And letting him treat her might make this a real date. Which felt like something she wasn't ready for.

She could fix something for them in the kitchen, but didn't want to get up in case he didn't snuggle with her again.

Louis picked up his phone and began tapping and scrolling. Her frustration mounted at the way he was distracted already—only a few minutes into hanging out with her. He'd gotten his kiss and was already losing focus. But when she looked over, she saw he was working his way through the online menu for the Watering Hole, the local saloon, which also served food.

"Would you like the house special pizza?" he asked. "Can you have gluten?"

"Maybe we could scrounge something from the kitchen instead." She sat up, but Louis tightened his arm around her, pulling her back in.

"I've got this. Large or extra large?"

"I won't be able to reciprocate next time."

Next time.

The phrase hung in the air between them, and she panicked. She was implying this might go somewhere.

"Chill, Hannah. Live in the moment."

"Their pizza is expensive."

"I invited myself over, remember?"

"You also rented the movie, as well as brought snacks and drinks." She glanced at his phone screen. "And delivery costs extra."

"I have it on good word from Maverick that the delivery guy is a college kid with a new baby. He could use the five bucks, since his scholarship doesn't cover diapers. And besides, neither of us is leaving this couch."

"We aren't?" she asked doubtfully.

"It's my duty to distract you, and I can't do that without pizza."

She waited in silence as he placed the order.

"Really? It's your duty? And you have to do it with pizza?"

"Well," he said slowly, "I could find other ways to distract you, but I'm not sure you'd be game." He gave her a wicked smile and Hannah gave him a playful slap on the chest, secretly pleased with his teasing.

She shifted so she could face him better. "You would know that I only do relationships. I'm not a side adventure."

"But you've given up having relationships?"

She looked away, gnawing on her bottom lip.

"So we've found a gray zone?" he suggested.

She wanted to give in and live in the moment, as well as in his arms. But to do that would mean learning to let go, which wasn't easy for a mom. Everything she decided about her own life had a direct impact on her boys, especially something big like this.

Louis shifted, tugging her left foot out from where she'd tucked it under her. He placed it in his lap and began kneading the ball, gliding his thumbs over the arch. She let out a moan of contentment.

"Right there?" He glanced up as he moved back to the spot that had made her groan.

Hannah nodded, letting the hitch in her shoulders loosen. She allowed herself to unspool, movie forgotten as she sagged against the cushions. A rebellious part of her wanted to stake a claim on the night, to studiously avoid considering the possible consequences of kissing and snuggling with a man who wanted things she couldn't understand.

"Gray zone, huh?" she mumbled, her muscles releasing their tightness as his thumbs worked their magic.

"We don't have to define our moments together. We have time to explore without the fear of hurting or confusing your boys."

Her lips curved upward. "Know what, Louis?"

"Hmm?"

"I've always felt gray's an underrated color."

It was nearly midnight when Louis slipped back into his shoes to head home. He could see Hannah shifting, tightening up. She'd let go, allowed him to treat her to pizza, kiss and cuddle her. But now she was obviously worrying about how to minimize his expectations.

Tonight it felt as though his luck, which had been amazing since the day Miranda Fairchild had hired him to coach her NHL team, the Dragons, had been building momentum. To have Hannah in his arms had made him the luckiest man he knew, and if there was one thing he could give her—even if he was unable to hold her for as long as he desired—it would be to open the shutters on her world so she could have the life she so richly deserved.

That's what he told himself. But in reality he wanted to hold her forever. Every moment and every kiss tonight had solidified that conviction, until he was now more certain than he had been of anything else in his life.

"Thank you for coming over," Hannah told him. "You were a pretty good stand-in for my boys."

Louis cast her a glance from the corner of his eyes as he zipped up his jacket.

She opened the door and flicked on the porch light. The timers had turned off her Christmas decorations hours ago, leaving Frosty deflated in the dark and making the night look like any other. Cold, slightly dreary and definitely lonely.

She was putting distance between them with her goodbye, possibly even discounting the connection they'd had between kisses. It made him wonder if she was going to pretend tonight had never happened.

"Feel free to invite yourself over anytime," she added, still holding the door.

Behind her, Obi rolled over on his living room bed and let out a sigh so loud it could be heard from the doorway.

"I have to work tomorrow, but I'm sure you can think of a reason to get me to come over and help you cope tomorrow evening, too. I'll be home for a bit between five and sevenish." Louis gave her a sly smile, hoping she'd find it slightly intoxicating. Or at least make her want to roll up onto her toes, grab his face and kiss him.

"I have no fun plans tomorrow night," she said, arms wrapped around herself. "Just work."

"At the day care?"

She shook her head. "A surprise for Wade. I'm going to paint his room while he's away. So unless you want to help me, I suggest you pretend the team has a very late practice, and then go catch a beer with the guys at the Watering Hole."

"Do you have everything you need? Paint? Brushes? Drop sheets?"

"You don't need to help. I'm sure you don't get many evenings off during the hockey season."

He gave a casual shrug. It was true, and tomorrow night he had the fundraiser gala the team's charity was hosting. But he'd skip that for her. Or make one of those late appearances, bid on a few things and head back home again.

"Good night, Louis."

As she closed the door behind him he wished for the day he wouldn't ever have to leave.

5

Hannah yawned as she walked home from the library. She'd spent most of the morning prepping Wade's room for the first coat of paint. Then she'd gone down to the library and met with the concert committee to set the song order, finalize the decorations and organize more volunteers to bake goodies and put together treat bags.

She zipped her collar against the wind, planning what she'd make for an early supper. She'd eat, then set to work painting.

As she came within sight of Louis's empty driveway, she felt a jab of disappointment. Which was silly. She knew he wouldn't be home until around five, and it was only four.

Loneliness hit her hard. Empty house. No friendly smile next door. She sighed and continued up the walk, letting herself in and Obi out. She hung up her jacket with determined care before letting the dog back in again.

Calvin and the boys had video-chatted with her earlier, Thomas scowling and jet-lagged. But Calvin was optimistic about all that France could hold for the four of them, and so she'd simply nodded and smiled.

Maybe she wouldn't get accepted into the education program.

Maybe she would move to France and love it.

But if they were seriously considering Paris, then why did she have a stash of painting materials currently sitting in Wade's bedroom? The paint was custom tinted, making it non-returnable. Why put money into a house she might soon be selling? Why apply for a program she might not be able to enter?

Entering Wade's room, Hannah knelt down, pried open a can and considered the color. Better than the room's current beige, but was this the right shade of blue? It looked so...permanent and decisive. There would be nothing subtle about this change. But she'd already filled boxes with stuffed animals, LEGO and an impressive amount of drawings, in preparation for painting. There was nothing left to do but put the new color on the walls.

Obi clacked down the hallway, his nails falling silent as he came onto the drop-sheet-covered carpet beside Hannah. He nudged her with his nose, then slid his wide, furry head under her arm.

"Hey, buddy." Their morning walk had been a bit shorter than usual due to the way she'd intentionally filled her day to keep busy, and the guilt hit her. It would be dark soon, too dark for her to truly enjoy walking him, but she could paint all night.

"Come on, let's go." She closed the can and leashed him up.

When she returned home just before five, having stopped several times to chat with neighbors, Louis's truck was back in his driveway. Home early? She felt a goofy smile brighten her face when she saw a note tacked to her door with duct tape.

Louis?

With a bounce in her step she called out a cheery hello to inflatable Frosty the Snowman as she passed, heading directly to the front door to pull down the note.

I should get your phone number. The Chinese food I ordered is getting cold. If you're hungry you know where to find me.

Hannah tried to fight her grin and lost.

Oh, she was hungry all right. Not just for the meal, but for the companionship and having a man look at her like she might be something he'd want to consume.

Her head popped up. Whoa. Where had *that* thought come from?

With burning cheeks, she reread the note. Louis still had that same scratchy, barely readable handwriting he'd had in high school. She'd been certain their group labs done in chemistry would fail because of his illegible scrawl and had insisted she write out every report herself.

For a moment she stood on her steps, undecided. She was playing with fire. People didn't change, and he'd been the thorn in her side all through school, a man who wanted and valued different things. If she went over to his place—like she wanted to—would she be getting into something she had no intention of pursuing?

But if she didn't go over...

Empty house. Soup for supper. Painting a room blue. Alone.

Ugh.

She wanted to spend time with Louis. To poke at him and be poked back. To laugh and kiss and carry on like she hadn't with a man in a very long time—since high school chemistry class, minus the kissing, in fact.

Plus she had to admit she was really curious about where this new friendship between them might go.

Unlocking the door, Hannah unleashed Obi and set him free inside, fighting the doubts racing through her mind. Before she followed him in, a familiar voice called from next door, "Your furry Jedi master is welcome if he wants to come, too."

Hannah leaned over the porch railing to get a better look at Louis's house. He had opened his screenless kitchen window and was hanging out to chat. It was so old-school she had to laugh.

She really needed to give that man her phone number.

"Okay," she hollered. "Can I bring anything?"

"Do you have any more cookies?"

She shook her head.

Mrs. Fisher, the waitress from the Longhorn Diner, was out walking her dog and she paused, her gaze moving from Hannah to Louis and back again. "Has Calvin gone to France?"

"He'll be back on Tuesday."

Mrs. Fisher knew that. She knew everything that went on in Sweetheart Creek. She was fishing for gossip.

"Do you have the night off?" Hannah checked her watch. Dinner rush. She should be at the diner.

"I do."

"Not even any gingerbread men?" Louis called.

"Actually, I might have some muffins in the freezer. I can…donate some—for you to take to the concert," She added the last part quickly, hoping Mrs. Fisher wouldn't get the wrong idea about her and Louis. All that was happening here was friendship. With the odd kiss thrown in.

"I didn't realize you were dating again," Mrs. Fisher said with a sly smile.

"I'm *not* dating." Hannah could hear the indignation in her voice, and then Louis's window slammed shut.

The woman nodded, her expression utterly unconvinced as she continued on with her dog.

Hannah glanced at Louis's closed, vacant window. She told herself it was just an old window that needed a lot of force to be opened and closed, and that the slam wasn't indicative of how she'd inadvertently offended him. Because he wasn't dumb. He should understand that whatever it was that they were playing at, it was never going to be real.

In other words, there was no reason to tell anyone about their confusing little gray zone because they'd only assume it was something more than it ever could be. This was nothing more than a temporary distraction for both of them.

Louis could see that his house was different from what Hannah had expected. He'd taken great care to make the place feel like a home. His home. No mismatched, tatty furniture placed haphazardly throughout the rooms. Nope, his mismatched furniture was arranged in cozy, welcoming groups with area rugs and even some healthy houseplants sharing space with coasters and magazines on side tables.

"That's the Mendenhall Glacier up in Alaska," Louis said, as Hannah paused to take in the largest of his framed photos. His favorite were the glaciers, their blues and whites somehow making the place feel spacious and open instead of cold.

"It's nice." She whistled, calling back Obi, who

had been trotting from room to room, lifting his nose to take in all that each space had to offer on an olfactory level.

"I just about fell out of the helicopter taking that one." Louis pointed to another photo, feeling strangely awkward. There'd been no kiss hello, no embrace. Where did they stand? He watched her pale pink lips, her brown eyes, waiting for a clue.

"Are you serious?" she asked, turning on him, hands on her hips as if preparing to scold him.

He grinned. There was the reaction he knew. He sidled close, allowing his arm to brush her shoulder as he stood beside her, looking at the image. He rested a hand on her waist. "I was getting ready to ski, and I popped my camera out from under my coat to take a quick shot just as the pilot pitched the helicopter to bank and land. I wasn't supposed to be leaning out like that."

"Always up for an adventure, aren't you?" The usual bite wasn't in her tone, and he got the feeling she was distracted, maybe even wishing he'd break the ice and kiss her.

"I guess so." He gazed at the picture for a second longer. He did like adventure. Mostly because after his mom had passed he'd preferred moving to staying still. If he sat, he thought. He felt. And there had been no end to how much he could feel.

"Do you sell your photos?"

He shook his head.

"What made you want to become a pilot? The rush of adrenaline? The ability to lift off and go where nobody else could? The imminent and constant pull of death or something like that?" She was smiling, uncertain, but sounded more curious than judgmental.

"My dad used to fly. It always seemed..." He paused as though searching for words, and Obi nudged his hand, earning an absentminded ruffling of his ears.

"Romantic? Adventurous?"

"It's a shift in perspective. You lift above everything, and suddenly all that stuff weighing you down doesn't matter anymore. It's down there and you aren't."

Hannah mulled that over, as though unsure about what could possibly weigh down the man she saw representing freedom and adventure.

"What do you run from?" she asked.

He gave her a funny look. "It's all still there when you land."

"Like what?"

He could tell he'd disrupted the entrenched

view she had of him as someone with an easy-to-discard adventure addiction. But he wasn't quite sure she was ready for his deeper side, a side she might be able to identify with or ache over.

"The things you want but can't have," he said quickly, moving to the kitchen. "Hungry?"

She followed him, caught his eyes and looked away.

She stopped in the middle of the tidy space. "This is just like Calvin's kitchen."

"Excuse me?"

"Well, no. Not really. He has necessities. This is a *home*. But it has a similar layout."

Louis got out plates and opened the boxes of Chinese takeout on the counter.

Calvin. Seriously.

Louis wanted to pull Hannah into his arms and give her a passionate kiss, then ask her if Calvin could do that. Send sparks shooting down their bodies, and make the world disappear like it did whenever they kissed. But unless the answer was a negative, he didn't want to hear it.

"I should be painting." She tipped a container, looking at its label. "Where did you order this? Sweetheart Creek doesn't have Chinese."

"I brought it from San Antonio. Should still be warm."

She opened the box and almost gasped when steam escaped. "It is! But…the city's over an hour's drive!"

"Who said I drove?" He grinned and started heaping their plates with food. Then he leaned close and dropped a kiss on her lips. Short. Sweet. And unexpected enough that she didn't have time to react. Then he sat at the table as if nothing had happened.

With her eyes sparkling, she shook her head, muttering to herself, "He flew to work. He *flew*. To *work*. Talk about an alternate universe."

Louis chuckled. He could see his life from her point of view. He worked with famous hockey players and commuted in a plane. He spent a lot of time traipsing across the continent for games, too. Romantic, unsettled, full of adventure.

But sometimes a man just wanted a home to come to at the end of the day. A partner who'd help him unburden. Who'd share laughs and meals, and basically help it all mean something.

"Do you like Exploding Kittens?" he asked, using a fork to eat his lemon chicken.

"The card game? Thomas adores it. Wade not so much."

"Yes, but do *you*?"

Hannah shrugged. "Wade tends to get close to

meltdown whenever he picks up the exploding kitten and doesn't have a diffuse card. He's still unfamiliar with the art of losing gracefully. Sometimes playing the game requires a lot of parenting."

"Want to play?" Louis waved the box of cards as she joined him at the table with chopsticks instead of a fork.

Her chair wobbled as she pulled it closer to the table, and he apologized, suddenly wishing he'd put some of his salary into appearances and newer furniture.

"It's reassuring." When he stared at her in confusion, she explained, "Your house and life are perfect and so different from mine. It's nice that there is something...I don't know...real."

"Ah."

She took a mouthful of chop suey before grabbing the deck to deal their cards. "First one to explode loses!"

Obi trotted over and dropped at her feet, his eyebrows doing a dance as he watched first Louis, then her.

As they played, they ate, the food going down fast. "I haven't had Chinese in over a year," she said.

"Hmm." He stretched one socked foot out, letting it rest against Hannah's. She didn't move hers away and he caressed the side of it with his toes.

She pulled her foot back. "That tickles."

"Sorry." He glanced under the table, but it was now out of reach.

Partway through the game, Louis pushed his empty plate aside and asked, "Why did you want to become a doctor?"

Hannah shrugged, keeping her eyes on her cards as she reached down to massage behind Obi's ears.

"Afraid to tell me?" he asked casually. He'd picked up an exploding kitten and groaned. He had a defuse card, though, putting the kitten back into play and saving him from losing the game.

"It was just something I wanted," she said, matching his easy tone. "You know how teens are."

"Teens want to help sick people?"

"Being able to heal someone is a big deal. When else do you get to positively influence someone's life in such a way? You get to help return them to normal after something as potentially massive as a brush with death."

They played another few turns before he said,

"You must've been devastated, not going to med school."

She tucked her lower lip into her mouth. He could see that the loss of her dream still stung.

Maybe, like he suspected, nothing had filled the hole left behind.

"You know, nobody seemed to even notice or care when I changed my dreams." Hannah folded her cards facedown on the table. "I expected it to be this big deal, and everybody just kind of acted like...like nothing had happened. Like it was a relief I was getting married instead and that it was *better* that I wasn't going to med school."

"I cared," Louis said.

He'd heard Mrs. Fisher and Hannah's mom talking in the diner after Hannah's fainting spell in class. Her mother had stated that it was good Hannah wasn't going to medical school. No stress from having people's lives in her hands on a daily basis. No massive student loans to break her. She'd seemed genuine in her relief, and it had made Louis feel for Hannah all the more.

"I've seen women trade their dreams for family before. It, uh, can't be easy."

"It wasn't about Calvin!"

"Okay."

"Did you not see me almost faint in my yard?"

She was pointing toward her house. "Or catch me in biology class?"

He fingered the cards in his hand, not looking up. Catching her had scared him. Not because she would have hit her head on the counter if she'd fallen, but because he'd been that tuned into her that he'd noticed something was wrong and was reacting before he could stop and think. And then holding her limp body in his arms—that had been freaky, too. She'd seemed so infallible and tough, and to see her like that had been alarming.

"I think everybody gets wrapped up in their thinking sometimes. They don't see all of the options." He picked up a new card from the pile and revealed it. Another exploding kitten. "No defuse." He slid his cards into the discard pile, having lost the game. "As for your friends, sometimes people don't see what others are going through."

After gathering all the cards together, Hannah reshuffled the deck, then set it aside. "You know why I didn't become a doctor. So why did you act like I'd given up? You all but implied that I was latching on to Calvin because I was giving up out of fear. That I'm too weak or too unambitious, and that it's to my own detriment. That when things get difficult I roll over."

Her voice had grown louder and she'd stood up, likely not even aware that she had. Obi pressed his nose against her thigh and she unclenched her fists.

"*Did* you give up?" Louis asked, his tone careful and quiet.

"No! I tried to change, okay? I tried self-hypnosis. I borrowed audiobooks from the library to listen to every night. I did everything I could think of to try and get over the fainting issue. I even had this whole mantra about how everything was okay even if somebody was bleeding. None of it worked. I *tried*."

Louis reached forward and touched her hand, and she yanked it back. "Giving up those scholarships was the hardest thing I ever had to do. And I hate that you think I hit a roadblock and gave up without even trying. I was *crushed*."

Louis lowered his head, trying to block out memories, pain. "I'm sorry. It's none of my business."

"So the things you pick on about me suddenly aren't your business because you might have been wrong? Because I'm making you uncomfortable?" she snapped. "We're *friends*, remember? We're open books."

"Would you still have married Calvin if you

didn't faint?"

She didn't answer, just took her plate and put it in the dishwasher. He wasn't sure if she was giving herself space to think and breathe, or getting ready to leave.

"You're the only one who ever challenged me about swapping med school for a wedding band," she said at last. "You know that?"

"Maybe it's because I cared more than anyone else."

She let out a bitter laugh. "Yeah, right."

"Maybe I *saw* how much you wanted to become a pediatrician and knew that you needed more than marriage to fill you up. Maybe because I've seen women give up their careers and their dreams for men who love them." He unclenched his hands, which had curled into fists on the tabletop. "Love isn't enough to fill the hole, and I've seen it kill people. Is it wrong that maybe I wanted more for you?"

The fire was back. Like the flame that had licked behind every fight they'd ever had, but today it felt big enough to consume them both if let out of control.

"And maybe I just wanted you to be happy for me—because it was my choice." Her voice was choked with tears.

"And maybe I could see that you weren't entirely happy with that choice."

She inhaled sharply through her nose. "Maybe my happiness is none of your business."

"Maybe I want it to be."

"How, Louis? It's always a fight with you. The good times will always lead to yet another fight because you refuse to step back and understand me."

She was in the doorway, her pretty brown eyes flashing at him. He looked away, knowing it would be easier to speak, to explain, if he couldn't see her.

"My dad traveled with the military as a pilot," Louis said. "My mom used to be the chief financial officer for Cohen's Blissful Body Care in South Carolina—somehow managing her career despite how we moved around from base to base. She loved it. She was made for it. But she gave it up for my dad. For me."

"She wasn't happy at home, and she got sick. She became a shell..." He paused and swallowed, then forced himself to meet Hannah's eyes. "You *have* to fulfill your dreams. You *have* to pursue life. You can't waste it. You can't let someone else run it all."

He stood, meeting her in the doorway. "Let

absolutely nobody stand in the way of what you want, Hannah. Nobody."

* * *

The kitchen felt small, electrified, as though if either one of them took a step they'd bring the walls down.

Hannah stood in the doorway, frozen to the spot. As a teen, Louis would get like this sometimes. He'd tighten up, become extra snippy with her, then skip chemistry class. But there was no class to skip now, and she was in his house. His doorway.

She'd been the one ready to flee this time, but now there was no way she'd give him the satisfaction. Not even with him facing off with her in the enclosed space. His eyes were a churning sea of emotion, and he reached out, scooping his hands into her hair, tangling his fingers in the strands, bracing her entire being for one long glorious moment before locking his lips on hers in a fervent kiss. He took Hannah's breath away with the intensity and ferocity of his need. She kissed him back, lost in the feeling of being consumed.

Panting, they broke apart.

"I hate you," she breathed.

He pulled her in for another long kiss, this one slower.

"I'm not your mom!"

"I know."

"I couldn't become a doctor," she whispered.

"I know."

"And it nearly broke me."

"I know that, too."

She rested her forehead against his chest. The muscles under his shirt were unfamiliar, but reassuring and solid. This man in front of her—the same one who'd tried to tune a piano—wasn't the Louis she thought she knew. He wasn't the teen she'd known in high school, and she was afraid to confirm the hunch that was developing within her. But it was like a blaring horn, disturbing her thoughts, reminding her that she'd never actually known the real Louis. And she might really, really like that version.

He'd seen the things she'd refused to. He'd seen that Calvin couldn't fill that big, empty hole inside her that losing her dream had created. In that context, she understood why he'd been so belligerent and prickly about Calvin.

But she also saw things that Louis refused to.

"This isn't going to work," she whispered.

He tipped her chin up, kissing her again, that

urgent need rising between them once more. It made her light-headed while at the same time grounding her. She felt lost, but found. It was as though two contradictory universes were spinning through her, and she was powerless to do anything but turn with them.

"Don't sell us short," he said between kisses.

"You put up walls," she retorted, kissing him back.

He pulled away to look at her. "What does that mean?"

"You run to a new adventure instead of sitting through the quiet. You fight instead of bonding."

"We're not fighting."

"That doesn't make it any less true."

His kisses had turned tender, his hands secure on her back, her waist. "What if you met someone who could love you the way you needed? What would you do?"

She leaned back. "What are you saying?"

"I think you could be a lot happier, Hannah Murphy—"

"I'm happy enough."

"—and I want to make it so."

"I said I'm happy!"

"You have everything you want in your life?"

His eyes were on her lips as he brushed the hair from her cheek.

"I applied to go back to school."

She shut her eyes. She shouldn't have told him that.

Now that he knew, he would never let her reverse her decision about going if she got accepted.

"Good. Don't give up on what *you* want. Don't put the needs of others—"

"Your mom's history is not repeating itself through me, Louis."

He dropped his arms, his face suddenly expressionless.

"Seriously, Louis. Let me live my life my way. They're my mistakes to make."

He took a step back, and Hannah floundered, unsure how to navigate. Had she crossed a line? Were there even any lines with Louis? If she'd hurt him, this was new and uncharted. They fought and threw daggers without injury. But right now it felt as though she'd found landmine territory, an area that could cause wounds. And she was mapless, unsure how to avoid them. One moment it felt as though he was throwing bombs at her feet, shrapnel and dirt flying up at her. The next moment he was pulling her out of harm's way. Could she do the same for him?

"Maybe I'll take the classes. Maybe I won't. I don't need to decide right now."

"Don't put others first, Hannah." His tone was quiet, full of warning.

"You do understand how disruptive going back to school will be—could be?"

"Tell me about France."

The air left her lungs.

France was a problem. One she didn't want to talk about with Louis.

"It's beautiful." She had unconsciously crossed her arms, a bad habit that seemed to rear up around Louis a lot, and now she lowered them to her sides. "There are job opportunities for engineers. The people over there speak French, and their food is supposed to be divine." She gave a defiant toss of her head.

"Tell me about how *you* feel about France."

"I don't want to move there," she blurted. *Dang*.

"Then don't."

"Yeah? And how's that going to work?" Tears of frustration and anger filled her eyes. "I'm a mom. I don't get to be self-centered, Louis. And maybe your mom didn't either. Being part of a family means being well-acquainted with give-and-take. Maybe she stayed home because she loved you, and being your mother was what mattered most to her. Maybe getting sick was unrelated."

"You have a choice, Hannah."

"My choices impact others."

"And theirs impact you."

She turned, striding toward the door.

As she fumbled into her boots, Louis stood close enough to touch. She looked up at him with an ache in her chest, afraid that if she made a peep it would unlatch the gate holding back the tears she was fighting.

"If something isn't working for one family member," he said, "chances are it won't be working for everyone else before long."

Hannah shakily zipped up her jacket, but before she could march out the door, Louis swept her into a hug, enclosing her in his warmth, his heart pounding under her ear. "Don't be like me. Don't run away."

"I thought you *wanted* me to be like you," she said in a choked voice, "and have the world bend around me."

He didn't answer, just kissed her with a tenderness that confused her even further.

6

"I'm coming, I'm coming."

Louis could hear Hannah through her door, grumbling away. He heard the lock slide back, but the door didn't open for a full twenty seconds.

Obi wasn't even barking.

Just when Louis was starting to grow concerned, it opened and a sleepy Hannah squinted against the weak morning light.

"You again?" she asked in a sweet, groggy voice.

Obi slipped past Hannah and leaned against Louis's legs, his big doggy eyes adoring as he waited for some love. Louis scratched his ears.

"Don't you ever sleep?" Hannah complained.

"Not much, no."

She huffed, obviously unimpressed. Most people thought it was cool how little he slept, imagining how much he could get done. He did a lot with his life, but that was to fill the gaping hole of those extra, empty hours.

Last night, at least, he'd had the gala to go to. Secretly, he'd been hoping for some way to swing Hannah into being his last-minute date, but that hadn't happened.

"You're cute when you're all sleepy." He handed her an insulated cup of coffee.

"Don't you understand fighting? You don't just come over the next morning as if everything is good again." She hoisted the cup like she was toasting him, and went to swing the door shut.

Okay, so apparently there hadn't been enough hours between their tough words and his coming over in order for her to feel sorted out again. He'd noticed her lights had still been on when he'd arrived home at one in the morning.

Probably painting. Probably fighting with him in her head.

He got it. She wanted to go to France to be with her family.

But she didn't want her family to go to France.

And she also didn't want to hold anyone back from having the life they wanted.

And yeah, he planned to pester her without mercy if she didn't pull the plug on leaving the country.

Louis stopped the door from closing. "I have a surprise. Put on some clothes."

Hannah narrowed her eyes, but didn't budge.

He tilted his head to the side, watching her for a moment. "I'm sorry if I was bossy last night."

"I'm happy, Louis."

"Okay."

"And I won't take back my words. About any of it."

"Fine."

They stood in silence. Not even the birds that liked to sing in the oaks lining their street had anything to say.

"So?" Hannah asked, eyebrows lifted.

"We're good?"

"No, we're not *good*. And I've created some mighty big plans around how to avoid you for the next few days, weeks, maybe even months! So git. Scram. Go crawl back under your rock."

"Hannah, I'm sorry if I pushed it too far. I just want what's best for you. That's all, I swear. I thought you needed a supportive push."

The anger left her face, only to be replaced with exasperation.

"What?"

"You really don't know how to fight, do you?"

"What do you mean?"

"Moving past fights isn't supposed to be this easy."

"But that's our thing, isn't it? Fight and get over it so we can fight again." He grinned. "And now maybe kiss a few times between battles?"

"Where's the guilt trip for how I treated you? This is where you can act all wounded and draw out your hurt forever, you know."

"Why?"

"It's what..." She seemed at a loss for words, her frustration mounting.

"It's what Calvin does when you call him on his crap?" She didn't reply. "I'm not Calvin."

"I know!"

"Then don't expect me to act like him when we fight."

"Fine. I'm sorry."

"Let him have his own baggage. He doesn't belong in our relationship."

"We're not—"

"We'll have plenty enough between the two of us without carrying his, too. The reason you and

I work is because we call each other out. And we let each other speak our thoughts. We don't carry our wounds like some sort of earned badge for our sash. That's what I love most about this gray zone we have, Hannah. We can be us."

"Okay." Her eyes were clear now, the sleep and frustration gone.

"And?" He could tell something was at the tip of her tongue, ready to be spoken.

"Don't meddle."

"Hmm." He looked down at his feet with a frown. He wasn't sure what her definition of meddling was, but he was fairly confident everything he said or did was some form of it.

He was good at meddling, but it almost always worked out. And sure, he'd gotten in a bit of hot water with his team captain Maverick Blades and the Dragons' publicist, Nuvella, for his recent efforts. But, again, it was working. Maverick was gaining more publicity and the beautiful woman he loved was on his arm.

Hannah sighed loudly. "So maybe I could handle making some changes in my life. You're right! Happy now?"

He peered up at her. Her shoulders had dropped and she looked like a kid who'd been caught eating all the cookies.

She groaned before admitting grudgingly, "School will be good. If I get in, I'll go, even though it'll cause a major mess."

She watched him carefully. He was supposed to say something now, but wasn't sure what. She was kind of admitting that his meddling was a good thing.

"So be happy you were right," she said, "and take your win on this one. Go ahead and gloat."

He resumed staring at his feet.

She sighed. "Oh, Louis. What did you do?"

He looked up. "How do you know I did something?"

"Mom radar works on grown-up kids, too."

"Well, to be fair, I didn't know about the no-meddle rule."

She waved the coffee cup he'd given her. "You're not going to let me enjoy this in peace, are you?"

He shook his head and took a step closer, so she backed into the house. "Go put some clothes on. And maybe bring a raincoat. Might sprinkle on us."

She sighed in defeat. "Fine. Give me a minute. I have to walk Obi-Wan anyway. We are walking, right?"

Louis shook his head. "Driving. But Obi can come and he can run around off-leash."

Hannah hesitated, then with a "fine" hurried farther inside the house. She returned moments later wearing faded jeans and a sweatshirt, her light brown hair wrangled into a high ponytail.

"Where are we going?" she asked, locking her door and passing him a dog leash.

"Trust me?"

She just laughed. He was going to have to keep working on that.

As Louis parked outside the community barn, Hannah knew that whatever his surprise was had to do with the piano.

"Calvin promised to deal with the piano," she said, as they made their way to the doors, a hint of rain in the air. Louis didn't need to know that her ex had given up already.

Louis unlocked the door, and Obi stood with his nose in the crack, ready to go in first, which he did as soon as it was open enough to shoulder his way in. Louis stepped inside and hit the light switches while the dog zigzagged along the wide plank floors that made up the dance floor, then beelined to the piano bench, giving it a thorough snuffling before moving on with his tour.

The piano was in shadow, not quite under one of the bright overhead lights. Hannah turned on the string of patio lights that crisscrossed the rafters above, deciding she'd better move the piano or bring a lamp on Christmas Eve.

Louis flipped up the piano keys' cover, then gestured for her to sit. "I was watching some YouTube videos last night."

Ha! So he hadn't had a perfect night's rest, either, even though she'd seen him zip out in a tuxedo only an hour or two after their fight. Somehow the idea that he hadn't slept much made her feel better.

She'd spent a lot of time fuming at him last night. First for being bossy, then for being right, and even—most infuriating—for him being so dang striking in his tuxedo when she couldn't get closer than her window to get a satisfying eyeful of him.

"I still don't have all the tools or pieces I need, but see if this is any better."

Hannah hesitated, then slowly eased onto the bench. "You tuned the piano?"

"You be the judge of that."

How did he have time to fight with her, feed

her, coach an NHL team and learn how to fix a piano? The man had some sort of time machine that gave him more hours in a day than anyone else.

Hannah poised her fingers over the keys, not sure what to expect other than disappointment. She inhaled, then let out the breath as she began playing a carol she'd soon be performing on Christmas Eve.

When she finished, she ran her fingers up the keys once again, noting that the dead one was still silent.

"I ordered a new key," Louis said. His arms were crossed over the top of the piano as he watched her, his shirt bunching at the shoulders as it curved around his muscles. "Did you know that they have piano graveyards, kind of like a wrecker for cars? You can order used parts."

"I didn't." The piano sounded surprisingly better. Was that because she had been expecting it to be awful, or had Louis actually improved its quality?

"What do you think?" he asked, when she continued to play.

"It's definitely better." She paused and tapped the silent key thoughtfully, then glanced up at him, startled by the intensity of his gaze. "Do you think the part will arrive in time?"

He shrugged. "Nobody will notice if you miss a note or play an octave or two higher or lower than usual."

Other than her poor singers, as they unconsciously tried to match the pitch. But she had to give Louis points for trying.

"Don't pour too much money into it." She sucked on the insides of her cheeks, mulling over the piano issue. Louis's fix might pass for one night. Although the missing key was annoying.

"Can you sing?" Louis asked, nudging her aside with his hip as he settled onto the bench beside her.

"What?"

He began to play a song that sounded disjointed and out of tune. In other words, perfectly Louis, as well as in sync with the old piano.

"What are you playing?" Hannah leaned closer, intrigued.

"You don't know it?"

She shook her head. The tune picked up tempo and she marveled at Louis's hidden talent. It reminded her of discovering a well-hidden chocolate egg a week after Easter—after you'd already eaten your stash and were craving another hit of chocolate.

He began singing, his voice low and gravelly. The kind that might fit someone eating a can of beans under a bridge, ready to scare you witless.

Wait. She knew this song.

"Tom Waits?" she breathed, as his fingers danced faster and faster. "Nobody knows Tom Waits."

And nobody knew how to play him on the piano. By heart.

Louis kept playing. "A girl in high school got me hooked."

Hannah frowned. She was quite certain nobody else in Sweetheart Creek High had been listening to this artist.

"I snuck a listen through her headphones when she went to the bathroom during chem," he explained.

"I knew I couldn't trust you." She started to sway as Louis continued to play "Just the Right Bullets." She was about ready to dive in as well, until he got to the second-to-last verse. The lyrics. The singer wanted the subject of the song to be happy. It was his only wish, and that he'd fix things for her—fix everything to make her happy.

She couldn't help but feel as though Louis had

chosen this song on purpose, and that it was saying more than she was willing to hear. She slid off the end of the bench, a lump in her throat.

"Nobody knows Tom Waits," she repeated, hugging herself as the lofty room echoed the song back at them.

Louis stopped playing, then smoothed dust off the keys. Neat and tidy. Black and white. Almost perfect.

"I do," he replied quietly.

But why?

"It's still out of tune."

"Getting closer?"

Hannah couldn't meet his eye. Couldn't quite consider the subtext, the deeper meaning behind his words.

And when had he learned to play piano? Piano like *that?*

She finally looked up, locking her gaze on his. "It has a ways to go before it'll be what I need."

As they walked from his truck to her door, Louis slowed his steps. He didn't get many days off during the regular hockey season, and he wanted to spend as much of today with Hannah as he could before tonight's away game. He wanted a chance to show her that maybe he was closer to what she was looking for than she realized.

"Come fly with me," he said.

"What?"

"Fly with me."

"Are you crazy? I'm not letting you fly me anywhere."

"Why not?"

"Because if I get mad I can't just get out and walk home."

Louis chuckled before realizing she might actually be serious. "Please?"

"No."

"I promise I won't fight with you. Although that might be very boring for both of us."

"I doubt a flying adventure with you could ever be boring."

"It's less risky than driving. Most days."

Louis loved being in the air. The freedom of it, the way his mind felt more open than it ever did while he was on solid ground. Ideas came to him. Songs and musical chords.

"What does that mean?" she asked doubtfully.

"Statistically, car accidents happen much more often."

"Have you ever flown anyone out of this grass-runway airport?"

"I have." Originally, he'd landed here with a woman in need of a safe place after an attack in the ocean town of Indigo Bay. Sheriff Conroy Johnson had found him in the right place at the right time. While Louis still didn't know much about the situation, he knew the woman had hidden out at a nearby ranch until things blew over. But that day, circling the familiar landmarks and then setting down on the grassy landing strip had brought back memories. Good ones that had made him miss the town and had stirred the desire to return one day.

"Come fly with me," he coaxed. "You'll like it."

"I'm still stuck on your claim that it's safe *most days*?"

Louis didn't reply, simply watched her debate playing hooky with the plans she'd already made for herself. He knew she had several days off. Most likely bored and alone. What could be more appealing than an adventure?

"Let's go play," Louis urged. "Let me show you the town from above."

"Today?"

"Yup. Right now."

He resisted the urge to check his watch. They

had time for a quick flight before he had to be in the city to catch a commercial flight to his game a few hundred miles away.

It was now or never—not just for his schedule, but for hers. Soon Calvin and the boys would be back and she'd have too many distractions and reasons not to go play.

"You think I need to run away from my problems?" she asked. The wind was toying with her ponytail, flicking strands that curled around her face.

"They'll all still be there when you land."

"You think I need perspective then?"

"Why can't you let loose?"

"Why do you always push?"

He shifted closer to her, under the large oak that bordered their properties. "Why do you always say no?"

"Why, Louis?"

"Because I want to see you smile."

She shot him a grotesque grin. "Satisfied?"

"Nope. It's not the same as your loving-life smile." He turned to walk back to his house. "I'll pick you up in ten minutes." He checked the sky. The clouds were moving along, leaving clear sky to the north. It would be beautiful up there.

"You're going to fly by and I'll jump in?"

He gave her a dry look. "Usually I'm the one being difficult, but maybe we should switch. You do it really well."

She was looking at the sky herself, frowning doubtfully.

"Are you scared?" he asked.

She didn't answer.

"Don't you deserve to have some fun and adventures of your own while the kids are away?"

He could see her softening, considering. He touched her elbow and said, "And if you're scared, you should know that as a pilot, I've never had a crash I couldn't walk away from."

She gave him a dark look. "You're impossible, and you make everything around you impossible. You're like Midas, except when you touch things they become complicated, just like you! But you know what? I'm taking you up on that plane ride, Mr. Adventure." She jabbed a finger in his direction. "But you have to pack our lunch, and I'm not paying for fuel."

He acted affronted. "It wouldn't be a very good date if I asked you to do that. Meet back here in ten or less."

Before she could protest that it wasn't a date, Louis cut across her yard into his own. He jogged up the steps and turned back to her with a wide grin before letting himself into the house.

There were no two ways about it. He was determined to secure a place in her inner circle whether she held the door open for him or he had to break it down himself.

7

"This is not a date," Hannah said, as Louis's plane lifted off the Sweetheart Creek airstrip. It was nothing more than a smooth pasture with a windsock, a few hangars that looked more like tractor sheds, and a barbed wire fence at the end of the runway to keep grazing cattle away.

She peered at the ground, which was growing farther and farther away. Flying in a plane this small—just four seats—was well outside her comfort zone. As was the implication that this flight might be a date. Was she so out of the loop that she didn't understand what dating was like beyond high school? Was dinner no longer a thing?

"You have to turn on your microphone," Louis

said, flicking a lever so they could talk through their bulky headsets.

Hannah stayed silent.

"What was it you said?" he asked, as they rose farther into the air, the big machine tipping in a gust of wind. There seemed to be a storm off to their right, the clouds tall and dark. Louis banked the opposite way, toward clear sky. She could feel him glance at her a time or two, but said nothing until they were above Cassandra's place.

He pointed down at Peppermint Lodge. "Looks like Cass is almost sold out of Christmas trees."

Hannah nodded and clung to the edge of her seat, refusing to look down at her friend's corral of live trees. What was she doing up here? She was a mom. She had children. She hadn't even verified that Louis had an actual license.

She ventured a peek through the side window, to find the ground racing away as they climbed toward the fluffy clouds and expanse of blue above. This was not natural. Humans should not fly. She pried her hands from the seat and clenched them into fists as she reminded herself to breathe.

Then suddenly they were zipping above the rolling slopes of Hill Country, not so close to the ground that she worried about hitting trees or disturbing wildlife, but high enough that it felt a bit scary.

She ordered herself to relax.

She ordered herself again.

"You'd better not crash," she said, her voice embarrassingly tight.

"Don't worry, I got my license to fly out of a cereal box." Louis winked at Hannah in a way that made her heart give a little flip and her cheeks warm. Despite their past, and despite their fights, she liked him. The problem was that she wasn't one to date casually—especially with her boys around—and with Louis it would never be anything but casual.

As they flew over a meadow, Hannah spotted a herd of deer pawing at the dried grass.

"Look!" she said, feeling the start of a smile. Hazy beams of sunlight shining down through the clouds made the meadow appear almost magical.

They rose higher. "Where are we going?" she asked.

"Do you always stress out when someone else is driving?"

"Just when I literally put my life in their hands."

"Trust me."

"Never."

"But we're on a date. That implies some level of trust, doesn't it?"

Hannah shook her head. Not a date. The gossip would be insane, and she so wasn't ready for that.

As she took in the sights below, she began to think about the divorcée memoir that Athena had given her. The author was learning to not care so much about how others perceived her and was daring to believe something new about herself post-divorce. Just because her marriage hadn't worked out didn't mean she'd failed and that there was something wrong with her. It was hard to accept that, to believe it for herself, but Hannah wanted to try.

And currently, it seemed as though everyone was trying to nudge her out of her sheltered shell, and to take some risks. But could she really let go? Could she move past the safety of the life she was currently living?

Hannah leaned back against the seat, eyes closed, concentrating.

Obviously, she felt there was room for personal growth, as she'd applied for school. But beyond that her mind went blank, refusing to answer anything further about her future.

She slowly opened her eyes to discover they were already near the windfarm one county over. Rows of white windmills waved lazily as they passed overhead.

Louis was watching her with concern, probably regretting taking her out, and worried she was either going to barf or was in the midst of a quiet meltdown. Maybe she *was* in a meltdown. She was melting down her old self-image.

They rose above a low bank of clouds and were suddenly blinded by sunshine. It was breathtaking.

"Wow."

"There's a little lake over here. I pass it on my way to work. There's a waterfall and sometimes I see deer drinking from the pond." He banked the plane to head in the direction he'd tipped his head, causing Hannah to squeal. It didn't feel dangerous, just different. It shook things loose in her box of internal worries.

They flew for several more minutes, Louis lowering the plane to show her his waterfall, before pointing out various hills, towns and landmarks like a guide.

She wondered if he'd decided to live in Sweetheart Creek so flying could be a part of his commute, giving him daily perspective. If he had, she understood why, because as he turned to head back home, the weight of her life was already pressing back in. All her so-called problems would still be waiting for her, just as Louis had promised.

"Lou, can we stay up here a bit longer?"

* * *

Lou. Hannah had shortened his name and had released her hands from their death grip on the seat.

"Hungry?"

"You did promise me lunch," she replied.

"I think you demanded it."

"It was part of the bargain to get me up here."

"I have an idea." There was a small town nearby, an hour from Sweetheart Creek by car, but it had an airstrip. He checked his watch for the time and date. Not too close to Christmas, so the food truck would probably be there today for the local flying club's taco brunch and meeting.

And the best part was that they'd be far enough away from town that they wouldn't set tongues awagging by showing up together. Because he wasn't dumb. He knew from the way Hannah had lied to Mrs. Fisher the other day about his muffin request being for "charity," that she'd have a negative knee-jerk reaction if anyone remarked on them eating out together. The woman still needed time to accept her change of heart where he was concerned.

The storm Louis had been watching was rolling closer, thunderclouds growing. They'd miss it, but in order to catch his commercial flight to tonight's away game, he'd have to scoot back into the air as soon as he dropped Hannah off in town if they made this stop.

He had time. No suit with him to wear to the game, but he could call his assistant coach and ask him to swing by the arena to grab the extra one he kept in his office at the rink, as well as his clipboard and game plan. At the San Antonio airport he could do a wardrobe change and he'd be right back on schedule.

Louis circled the small town, and as he'd hoped, spied a food truck in the little airstrip's gravel parking lot. He checked the wind, radioed with other pilots as there was no tower, and prepared for landing. Within moments they were touching down. It was a smooth landing, one of his best, with little turbulence to disturb the small plane despite the storm brewing within a hundred miles.

He began braking, then motored toward a spot near the hangars where they could leave the plane.

“Where are we?” Hannah asked.

“Lunch,” he said, pointing in the direction of the food truck. They climbed out of the aircraft, and he asked as he secured it, “Have I convinced you how awesome plane rides are?”

“It was nice.” Hannah paused, then added, “Actually, it was really great. Thank you.”

“You’re welcome. And as a first date bonus, that was another landing where everyone can walk away.”

“First date,” she muttered, but he could see she wasn’t actually upset.

He gestured to the taco truck as they drew closer. “Right, sorry. I forgot. You said this isn’t a date, but can I treat you to lunch anyway?”

“I thought you said you couldn’t hear me without the microphone thingy turned on?”

He smirked. Of course he’d heard her.

“How did you know this was here? Did you plan this?” She was watching him, a small smile toying at the edges of her lips.

He wanted to say he had, but gave a casual shrug instead.

"Thank you, Louis."

"You're welcome. But you don't need to thank me yet. You still have time to get mad at me and walk home from here. I'll warn you, though, it's an hour by car, so a bit of a leg stretcher."

Hannah laughed as they lined up for food. "Well, don't get me angry and I'll accept a flight home again."

The man in front of them, a familiar-looking pilot, nodded to Louis and shook his hand. "Tough season so far."

Louis grimaced. "Sure is."

"Game tonight?"

"Yup."

"Good luck." The man chuckled and faced the front of the line again.

Yeah, the Dragons might be becoming a bit of a joke with their losing streak. But his plan to turn things around was starting to work. He just needed time and patience.

"Do people recognize you often?" Hannah whispered, leaning closer.

"It happens."

Then, as though realizing where they were—on a date in the middle of nowhere—they smiled at each other, a giddiness growing between them. Louis felt like a teenager, and he liked how Hannah was unable to hide her growing grin.

"I feel like the kids at the day care when I told them Santa is coming to visit on Monday," she confessed.

"Yeah?"

"Garfield Goodwin is dressing up for us."

"Really?" The man would make a natural Santa. He had wild white hair and kind eyes. The kids would adore him.

"I love this time of year." Hannah gave a happy sigh, her eyes lingering on the colored Christmas lights strung on the food truck and the chef's crooked Santa hat.

The woman loved Christmas, and Louis hoped that some of her spirit would rub off on him. He hadn't felt very jolly about the season in a long time, but this year he had hope. And maybe someone to spend it with—his dad, now, of course, but maybe he'd see Hannah, too.

"Is this what your life is like? Just going with the flow?" she asked.

"I'm pretty scheduled with hockey, but when I can allow some space for spontaneity I seize it. You don't?"

"I'm used to controlling things so I don't have

children melting down on me. I'm not used to going with the flow."

"Do you trust me?" he asked.

Instead of answering right away, Hannah seemed to run through some sort of mental checklist. A fairly long one, he noted. But she finally said, "You come from a good place, even though you make me want to pull my hair out half the time."

"Do you trust me?" he repeated.

"Sure, to scramble my mind."

He laughed. Nothing came easy with this woman. And for whatever reason, he liked that. For all her people-pleasing personality traits, she sure could dish it out where he was concerned.

"I trust you to help Thomas." She was watching him now, her eyes filled with approval and warmth. "I can trust you to be kind to my dog. And I just climbed into a plane without seeing your license, and let you fly me up into the skies, opening my world to a whole new perspective."

Louis felt the impact of her words. As they moved forward in the lineup he faced her, his throat thick as he asked, "Is that a yes?"

She stood close to him, a flash of fire in her gaze. "You need to learn patience, Louie."

"Patience hasn't served me well in the past." Especially with her.

"Trust takes time. I'm not quick to give it, and even more so when it comes to you *and* me. I don't think I even know how much I trust you yet, but it's obviously quite a bit. Give me time to figure this out. But if you'd rather race off to the next thing..." She stepped back, palms raised. "I guess it's no big deal, Adventure Man."

How was it possible to get it wrong with her almost each and every time?

He inhaled slowly, trying to calm his mind, adjust his pace. To be present, to accept the gift he had. This moment. This suggestion from a woman he cared about.

"So you trust me."

"Yes, I do." Then she rolled up onto her tiptoes and kissed him.

* * *

Louis led them to a picnic table with their grouper fish tacos and iced tea. Despite the nearby storm it was nice enough to eat outside as long as they didn't linger.

Hannah wanted to ask about the dark clouds, but also wanted to show Louis that she trusted him. That she was okay being in the passenger seat and letting him be the boss.

As they dug into their lunch, she finally found herself unable to resist. "The clouds over there? Should we be worried?"

"I have an eye on it." He seemed worried, though, as if the weather was doing something he didn't like.

"You look concerned."

He took several bites of his taco, then calmly asked, "Do you have to know everything about everything at every moment of every day?"

"How many times can you say 'every'?" she quipped.

"Many, many times." He grinned and polished off his first taco. "Come on, Hannah. You said you trust me. Put those words into action." Despite the confidence in his tone, his eyes flicked to the sky, underlining the concern she saw growing in him.

Breathe. Enjoy. Relax. Go with the flow. She trusted him to stay grounded rather than to fly through a storm.

As she savored the tangy taco, the juices dripping down her hands, she allowed herself to be in the moment. A plane ride, a kiss and a picnic.

It was a date.

And she'd been the one to kiss him. She hadn't needed to, she'd wanted to. And so she had.

She was pretty sure that helped make this an official date. Going on one date did not mean they were dating, but it felt like it might be getting close to that.

"Good?" Louis asked, gesturing to her second taco.

"Love it." She took the last bite of her first and wiped her fingers on her napkin. "Would be even better with a margarita."

"Maybe one of these old-timers has a flask and we can turn this iced tea into something adult."

"Are you suggesting illegal public drinking?"

"Where's your sense of adventure? Have we already exhausted it?"

She peered into her plastic cup, then took a sip. "Well, you know me. If it won't send me to jail then it's not worth it."

"You enjoyed your one and only night in the clink?"

The high school horse dare. Of course he remembered that. Her one attempt at rule-breaking and she'd relied on a four-legged beast to help her get away with it.

"I wasn't in there all night." She hesitated, then

added, "I saw you across the street when I was released." She hadn't actually been arrested, but wasn't allowed to leave the station until her parents had claimed her and she'd made a plan to make amends, as well as fix the damage.

"I saw you, too."

"You were smirking."

"Because the perfect Hannah Murphy had done something that surprised me."

"That's not why."

"And because..." He was smiling up at the sky and she had a feeling it was at her expense.

"Riding a horse through the school is not funny," she said, quoting her mother.

"But it was, wasn't it?"

Hannah thought of her friends. The laughter. The memories. The adrenaline at doing something out of the ordinary, and breaking rules. Despite the fallout, she didn't actually regret it. "It was kind of fun."

"Want to go paint our names on the water tower?" Louis asked, the wind ruffling his hair as he tilted his head in the direction of Sweetheart Creek. "Relive some of our youthful energy?"

"No," she said definitively.

"Did I ever tell you that story of that guy—

whose cousin was he? Yours? He's from Blueberry Springs, way up north."

Hannah shrugged.

"Anyway, he fell off their water tower."

"And so you're suggesting *we* do that? Is this some sort of twisted Romeo and Juliet death pact thing?"

"No, not fall off it. I like adventure, but the kind I can walk away from." He watched her for a beat. "Come on, you must have heard the story. He was trying to impress a girl."

"Oh my gosh!" Hannah squealed, the memory coming back. "I do remember hearing that." She reached across the table, squeezing his arm as details came back to her. "From Daisy-Mae! She knows the story. She knows the girl he was trying to impress. Mandy something. She painted *his* name up there a few years ago and got busted like he did. She didn't fall off, though." Hannah released Louis's arm. "I heard they got married."

"I tell ya, pranks are the new I-love-you's of the dating world."

She sighed and rolled her eyes.

"What? Come on, that was almost funny."

Hannah took another sip of her iced tea. This whole day felt special—something she would always remember, and not just because it was their first official date. She lowered her cup to hide the tremors that were starting in her hand.

"Why were you really smirking at me?" she asked, realizing he hadn't fully answered her earlier question.

He shrugged, scooping up a bit of fish from his takeout tray and popping it in his mouth.

"You can't get out of answering by stuffing your face."

He chewed thoughtfully, then replied, "I wasn't actually smirking. I thought maybe you were rebelling. You know, about to change up your life. I was curious."

"Change it how?"

"It doesn't matter."

"Tell me."

His eyes got a faraway look as if he was lost in his thoughts, and Hannah wondered if teenage Louis had thought she was about to dump Calvin and find a way to become a doctor.

Louis's focus returned, and he said cheerily, "I was going to bail you out if your parents didn't."

Hannah shifted toward him, taken off guard by him changing the subject. But she didn't know what to say. Bail was not exactly a teenager's part-time-work kind of money. Not that her parents had needed to post it. Instead she'd gotten a lecture from every adult she knew, and had spent the next morning making things right again.

To think that Louis had been there to make sure she was okay was touching.

Especially since she'd spent every minute inside that jail cell thinking her parents weren't going to come, that they'd be too humiliated to claim her. She'd honestly believed they were going to let her sit there to learn the lesson she already knew: going with the flow and being a bit mischievous could land you in jail. Don't break the rules. Don't be anything beyond ordinary and steady.

She inhaled to steady herself. "Thank you," she said to Louis.

"I didn't do anything."

"But you were there." She clasped her hand over his, giving it a squeeze.

"I'm glad your parents came and got you." He turned his hand over so they were palm to palm, his fingers twining with hers. "It would have been pretty awkward when you rejected my help."

She laughed, knowing that was likely how it would have played out. "As much as I balked about today, I appreciate you convincing me to come."

"I'm glad you came." He looked at the sky, then

at her taco. "You want to finish that in the plane? Because it looks like we have a storm to beat."

* * *

Louis wasn't one to panic, but at the moment he was feeling pretty uncomfortable. The clouds were roiling and the storm was shifting, picking up to the point where flying back to Sweetheart Creek was no longer an option. At least not for another few hours.

He'd messed up.

He'd finally wooed Hannah into giving up control, into trusting him, and he'd mucked it up.

He checked the weather radar on his phone again. "You seeing this, too?" he asked, showing his screen to one of the other pilots near the hangars.

"That wasn't predicted." The man gazed at the sky. "You gotta head west?"

Louis nodded.

"Might want to wait a few hours."

"That's what I was thinking." Louis checked the screen again before looking up at Hannah.

"Are we stuck here?" she asked, her face growing pale.

"Anywhere you need to be today?"

She shook her head.

He checked the weather map again as drops of rain sprinkled over them. "Good. How do you feel about going with the flow and coming to a hockey game?"

* * *

Hannah barely had time to wrap her mind around their weather predicament before they were climbing back into the air, the increasing wind buffeting them as Louis banked away from the dark scary clouds. Lightning could be seen in the distance, toward Sweetheart Creek. There was no going home by plane until that storm was finished, and that wouldn't be for several hours. Hours Louis didn't have.

So suddenly Hannah was flying with him across state lines to his hockey game. He'd made a series of quick calculations, decisions and phone calls, and it was done. The efficiency of his planning and the shifting of their schedule to accommodate his responsibilities shouldn't have surprised her, but they did. He was calm, in control, and honestly, pretty darn sexy.

And she was going to an NHL game. As the coach's date. In a plane he was flying.

Life with Louis in it would never be ordinary, that was for certain.

"Are you sure you'll get there in time?" she asked.

He didn't reply for a moment, his steady, serious gaze on the instruments, then on the flashes of lightning in the sky behind them. It felt to Hannah as if he was pushing the plane faster.

"Yeah. You bet." His tone was casual, yet distracted.

She gave him a few minutes to put distance between them and the storm, and soon felt the plane settling as the turbulence waned.

"Do I wait at the airport for you until you're done?"

He looked at her in surprise. "I ordered a car and asked my assistant to get you a seat in the sky box. There will be players' wives and girlfriends, snacks, drinks and some VIPs up there."

Hannah looked down at her jeans and sweatshirt. "Maybe I should sit in the nosebleeds."

"You'll be fine. I think Daisy-Mae will be there."

Hannah cringed. Her friend was a former beauty queen who looked runway-ready even in her pajamas. But it would be nice to be able to sit with someone she knew.

It was a long flight, with Louis relaxing more and more the farther they got from the storm. But a new level of concentration set in as the sky darkened and they got closer to their destination.

"Are you thinking about tonight's game?"

He nodded.

"It's been a tough season."

Another nod.

"Will I be distracting if I'm at the game?" She grinned, well aware of the flirtatious tone she'd adopted.

He grinned back. "Very. That's why I didn't get you a seat down by the ice."

She laughed, then gasped as she looked west, catching sight of the sky, streaked with pinks, oranges and a band of purple as the sunset unfolded. "It's so beautiful!"

"Our own private show."

"I can see why you like flying. From now on I'm going to feel ripped off when I have to sit in the back of a plane, instead of the cockpit." And even more so when she wasn't with Louis.

* * *

Having Hannah in the sky box was proving just as distracting as having her in a seat near the players' box. All through the game Louis found himself glancing in that direction, as though he expected to see her watching him, even though it was too far away for him to make anyone out. He also began watching the Jumbotron above the ice, something he'd never done before, in case the cameras spanned to the sky box.

He even found himself winking at the unseen camera one of the times it panned to him.

"You looking to score a deal with a shaving company, Coach?" Landon asked at halftime, as they left the rink. The Zamboni would clean and resurface the marked-up, gouged ice while they held a team meeting in the locker room.

"Why's that?" he asked his goalie, rubbing his jaw to check for five o'clock shadow.

"You're playing to the camera. Winking and stuff."

"He wasn't on the plane," the assistant coach said pointedly.

"I flew myself."

"And a private guest, I hear?" Maverick, his captain, chimed in. "Looks like Coach has a girlfriend."

The men laughed, for some reason finding the idea humorous.

"Y'all going to focus on the game and get me a

win tonight so Miranda doesn't fire us all?" he retorted.

"Got to impress the lady," Landon cooed.

Louis gave him a level look. He hated to admit it, but he would love a win tonight. "I'll buy y'all Christmas gifts if you pull off a win."

"Oh, he's serious about this one."

"Who is it?"

Louis ignored the question and moved to the whiteboard in the locker room. "Listen up. Tonight we're turning up the heat and earning a W. And here's how we're going to do it."

8

It was Monday morning, two days after her date with Louis, and Hannah still couldn't stop smiling. On Saturday she'd done something spontaneous, something just for her. An adventure. And she'd loved it. Going to an NHL game—where her team won!—and sitting in the VIP area was incredible. As was taking a plane and hired car to get there—with the coach, no less. Being Louis's date had been fun. Surprisingly so.

Her friends were right. She needed more adventure. And Louis, even if he wasn't the type to settle down with a family, was the right man to help her heal from her divorce and learn to live and rediscover herself.

She'd practically stalked his house yesterday, even though she'd known he was away for practice and meetings. They'd had two away games in a row, and another tomorrow night. She wanted more time with Louis. More adventure. More surprises. More feeling special.

"Miss Hannah, how many sleeps until Santa?"

"Hmm? Oh." She brought herself back to the present, to work. With Christmas morning only three days away the kids at the day care were pretty much bonkers. And she loved every second of it.

Kneeling on the floor, Hannah took three-year-old Anya Elm's hands in her own and gently curled down two fingers. "This many sleeps until Santa comes to your house."

Anya wiggled and grinned.

"Do you think you can wait that long?" Hannah asked.

Anya shook her head and Hannah felt a twinge of sadness. Santa was supposed to come today, but Garfield Goodwin's girlfriend, Mrs. Fisher's twin sister, had called earlier to say he was down for the count with the stomach flu.

Hannah had called half a dozen people, searching for any male in the county willing to don the suit. She'd failed, and then had had to break the news to the kids. No Santa visit today. They'd taken it like troopers. Troopers who'd lost their platoon in a horrifying and grueling war.

Hannah had been about five seconds from grabbing the sack of gifts hidden by the door and putting on the suit. Or from calling Louis and begging him to abandon today's schedule and rescue her. But the man needed to sleep and work. On Saturday night they'd flown home late, not getting in until two in the morning. The last thing she'd wanted to do this morning was wake him up and ask for a favor. A favor she was certain he'd say no to.

So instead she'd moved craft time up by an hour.

"Maybe we could make some reindeer food," she said to Anya. "Have you done that before?"

The girl shook her head again.

"That settles it. Let's get the rest of the kids and make some reindeer food for Rudolph and his friends."

Like the little leader she was, Anya gathered up the few playmates whose families weren't yet on holiday, and they settled at one of the low tables to get started. There were only ten kids, which was fine for Edith and Hannah—when Edith wasn't busy in her office.

"Do you know what helps reindeer fly?" Hannah asked the children.

"Snowshoes!" replied April Wylder's five-year-old son, Kurt, who then burst into giggles.

"Ice cream," another said.

"Wings?" asked Anya.

Hannah held up a tiny container of glitter. "This does." She showed them a small plastic bag. "And they love oats. So what we do is we mix these two together, and then on Christmas Eve we sprinkle it out in the yard where you think Santa might land his sleigh, so the reindeer can eat it."

"I'm not allowed on the roof," said Kurt.

"Sometimes they land on our lawns," Hannah said, "and I bet if you put some in the front yard they'll eat it. They aren't always hungry, though. But that's okay, because the birds will eat it."

"Is glitter safe for birds?" asked Edith, the day care owner, as she glided by. She was like a harbinger of gloom, the way she coasted silently through the room, popping up to make Hannah doubt the wisdom of anything she did. How the woman had ended up running a day care was a mystery. Maybe if Hannah didn't wind up going back to school she'd look into ways to take over the business.

She looked at the container of glitter, double-checking that this was the stuff she'd bought from the grocery store's baking aisle. "It's edible."

The kids and she set to work on the reindeer food, and by the time they were done Hannah was yawning. She'd been up late painting last night, imagining what it might be like to date Louis Bellmore for real. And the night before she'd been out with him, unable to sleep when she got home as she'd been so dazzled by the life he had and how it was so unlike her own.

"Okay, put your reindeer food in your cubby," Hannah told the little ones when they were finished. Then find your stuffy to snuggle with. It's story time!"

Story time. Then nap time. Everything was right on schedule, the only way to keep a roomful of tykes from extreme meltdown.

The children circled around Hannah on the carpet as she opened their afternoon story about a snowman. But then the front door of the day care opened, bringing in a gust of wind. It was Anya's mom, Naina Elm, the principal of the elementary school. "Guess who I found outside?" she announced loudly.

Hannah did a quick head count, her heart hammering in her chest. None of the children were missing. But before she could ask who she'd found, a man came in dressed in a red-and-white suit.

Santa.

The kids went wild, storming the gate that separated them from the front entry, where Santa stood with Naina. "Santa! Santa!" they shouted. "He came! He's here! He's here!"

As Hannah joined the kids, Santa glanced up from the kids and familiar blue eyes greeted her with warmth. Her breath caught in her chest.

Louis.

* * *

Any lingering uncertainty about Louis dissolved, and Hannah could have sworn that her ovaries twitched as she battled the urge to swoon over him. Just a little.

There was something about having a man you kind of liked dress up as Santa to come and save your day. It was a noteworthy item on the mental does-he-check-out list.

Louis let out a booming "Ho, ho, ho!" and the children's excitement level ratcheted up another notch.

"I saw Louis and his dad at the Longhorn this

morning," Naina whispered in Hannah's ear. "When he heard you didn't have a Santa he offered to step in."

"He has meetings and a practice today," Hannah said with a frown. Was he skipping work for this? Was he going to scrape in—late, or almost late—because of her?

Naina was beaming at Louis in a way that made jealousy rise inside Hannah. "Naina, you're *married,*" she whispered.

The woman simply smiled.

Hannah supposed ovaries were ovaries, and why wouldn't hers be twitching, too?

"Seriously," she muttered to Naina.

Anya bounced over to them, squealing, "Mummy, Santa's here!"

Naina nodded at her, then continued whispering to Hannah. "Don't judge me. He's hot. Successful. *And* dressed as Santa."

True, true and true.

"And he's doing it for *you.*" Naina nudged her.

"Who is this?" Santa asked, coming closer to the baby gate that separated the entry from the play area in order to peer at Hannah. "Hannah Noelle?"

"How do you know my middle name?"

"I'm Santa! You live on Cherry Lane! And my,

you're all grown up. Do you have a boyfriend?" He was watching her with dancing eyes, and she felt heat rise in her face as the children giggled.

She might have to mentally uncheck a box or two on the does-he-check-out list if he continued on like this.

"Miss Hannah, kiss Santa!" Anya called, starting another round of giggles.

"There will be no kissing. Everyone move back so Santa can come in." Hannah began shooing the kids farther from the entry while Naina opened the baby gate for Louis. As soon as he was inside Colts and Fillies, he closed in on Hannah, asking, "Have you been a good girl?"

Seriously. One minute inside the day care and he was knocking everything off-kilter. Why did she find herself drawn to him? She must have something wrong with her brain.

"Okay, boys and girls," Hannah said, ignoring Louis, "go to the story-time carpet so Santa can show us what he brought for us." She tipped her head to the right, subtly gesturing to the sack of toys hidden from the kids' view.

Louis had it over his shoulder in seconds. "Speaking of presents, do you boys and girls want to know what I brought for Miss Hannah?"

Her head snapped to Louis. He was digging in

the sack of toys, and the kids all raced back to him. He had palmed a box roughly the size of a volleyball and was holding it over his head. "This present says it's for Miss Hannah. What could it be?"

"Me! Me! I want one, too!" Anya was bouncing in front of him, yanking at his sleeve as he tried to pass the gift to Hannah.

"There's one for you, too. Miss Hannah's been extra good this year, and she's often forgotten. Is it okay if she gets hers first?"

Anya nodded, and Louis handed Hannah the gift. "Go ahead. Open it."

Hannah reached for it, curious where it had come from. The look Louis was giving her suggested he'd somehow planted it in the sack. She hefted it, finding it heavier than she'd expected. What was it? Something over-the-top? Ridiculous? Embarrassing? Telling?

"I'll open it in a bit." She tucked the gift in the crook of her arm. "Let's get the kids settled." She eyed Edith's office, and sure enough, her boss came trundling out to see what the disturbance was.

"What's this?" Edith asked.

"Santa!" Anya yelled. "He came!"

The woman's eyes narrowed as she tried to identify the man behind the fake white beard.

"He's here now," Hannah said brightly.

"And he has a gift for Miss Hannah," Louis said with a wink.

"He does?" Edith's tone was unamused.

"He does," Louis said smoothly. He winked again, at Hannah's boss, whispering, "No gift for you. I heard you were *naughty*."

She jolted as if she'd been goosed, and Naina giggled.

"Open it," Louis urged, his attention back on Hannah.

"I will." She began directing the kids toward the carpeted area again, placing the wrapped box high on a shelf so they wouldn't open it on her behalf.

"Come, children," Edith said. "Let's gather on the carpet with Santa."

Hannah stood at the edge of the crowd, waiting to be needed as Louis expertly wrangled the little ones into a circle. The way Louis was so natural with them warmed her heart, and while she had no plans to fall in love again, and especially not with someone so frustratingly meddlesome, she could see that if she wasn't careful,

Louis might just sneak in and steal her heart, anyway.

"He's a sweetheart," Naina said, joining Hannah. "And he really likes you."

"Oh, I don't know," she murmured, desperate to pump her for details on why she thought that.

"He thinks very highly of you," Naina said. "In fact, I heard you'll be joining the teaching profession very soon."

"What?" Her head snapped away from Santa and the little fantasy that had been playing out in her brain. Louis had been wrestling sheets onto Thomas's bed, then tucking him in before joining Hannah for a cup of tea and warm kisses that tasted like love and chocolate chai.

Naina was smiling at her expectantly. "You're going back to school for a few classes to complete an education degree, right?"

Hannah had told only one person that she'd applied. One. And he was already blabbing it all over town, while she hadn't even been accepted into the program yet. That man did *not* understand the no-meddle rule.

"You chose a great school. They're well-rated for their elementary education program," Naina said. "Do you have your résumé or portfolio ready?"

Portfolio?

"No, not yet."

"Well, when you're ready for a job, let me know."

"It'll probably be a few years before I'm certified...."

"Oh." Naina looked taken aback. "I didn't realize you had that much upgrading to do."

"That's if I'm accepted into the program."

"Oh. I must have misunderstood." Her cheeks pinked. She was no doubt thinking about how Hannah had sworn up and down that she was going to become a doctor and then hadn't. Naina herself was the kind of woman who made plans, set goals and then burst past them ahead of schedule. She didn't veer, she didn't waver. She didn't fail.

Hannah struggled not to shoot daggers at Louis, who had all the kids hanging on his every word. That man really needed to learn to keep his nose out of her business. Not only was she now feeling as though she'd just entered an impromptu interview wholly unprepared, but he'd put Naina in an awkward spot, too.

"I've only just applied, but I'd love to work at the elementary school when I'm done." Hannah pulled her sweater sleeves over her hands, wanting to disappear.

"Do you know which grade you're hoping to teach?" Naina asked, her tone a little less enthusiastic and a bit more professional now.

She shook her head. "Not yet."

"Well, we're often looking to cover maternity leaves or in need of a substitute teacher here and there. We'll get your name on the list when you're ready."

"Thank you."

Completely unprepared.

* * *

He was in trouble now. Louis had caught the angry looks Hannah had been shooting his way earlier, and now she'd called him into the small staff room off the barricaded playroom.

Still dressed as Santa, he had been sitting on the floor surrounded by shreds of wrapping paper that Hannah had given up collecting after he'd suggested the kids rip up every little bit and throw it around like confetti.

Yeah.

He was that guy.

Naturally, the children adored him. Hannah… not so much.

Was it his fault he got caught up in their enthusiasm?

He'd thought he'd been doing her a favor, keeping them happy. There'd been no fighting or whining. And he did have a game to play when it was time to clean up the paper later. He wasn't planning to saddle her with a mess.

"What's up?" he asked, as he joined her. She closed the door and he glanced through the window that allowed them to peek out at the kids.

Hannah licked her lips and straightened her red Christmas sweater.

"You okay?"

She reached out and straightened the cushion over his flat stomach that was filling out his costume. She was tugging it like she wanted to rip it off him. And not in a good way.

"You told Naina I was going back to school," she said, still focused on his Santa suit. Her tone was flat. Dangerously flat.

"Yeah. It came up." He removed her hands before she ripped the red fabric. "She sounded excited."

"How did something like that come up?"

He'd meddled. That was how. And she was supposed to be too excited to notice.

"Did you like your Santa gift?" he asked.

"I haven't opened it yet."

Louis gave her an expectant look, which she ignored.

"Louis, there are boundaries to establish. And respect. We need that if we're going to make this work."

"Ah. No meddling. Ever." He scratched under his red hat, hoping he wasn't messing up his wig too much. He froze, replaying her words. "Wait. Make this work?"

Did that mean she was thinking of a relationship?

"Santa! Come see my train!" Elias hollered through the glass window. That kid was the best. If he ever had a son he hoped he was like Elias. But the boy's timing maybe wasn't so hot at the moment.

"Santa!"

Hannah sighed and gestured toward the door.

"Are we...?" Louis wasn't sure how to phrase his question. "You and I...are we something?"

"Santa! Santa!"

"Hang tight, Elias. I'm coming."

Hannah began physically steering Louis from

the room. He turned in the doorway, watching her for a moment. She was beautiful, even when frustrated with him. They'd had a good first date —the best he'd ever had—and today had been shaping up to be good, too. He hoped his slip-up hadn't ruined it all.

"No meddling," she said firmly.

He grinned.

"Louis! I haven't even been accepted into the education program." Hannah's frustration finally exploded and her words came out in a storm. "She was practically interviewing me for a job, thinking I was already looking. It took me off guard, and I gave her the impression that I'm completely oblivious and unprepared, and that I don't understand how any of this works!"

Before she could do anything other than suck in a fresh breath to continue her rant, Louis shut the door again, pulled down his fake Santa beard and kissed her like it was his last chance.

Which he hoped it wasn't.

Moments later he released her limp body, now devoid of anger.

He really needed to have her happy with him because he'd seen an article online speculating that the mystery woman in the sky box was his girlfriend. He wanted Hannah to be pleased about that, but he wasn't certain she was ready to claim the title, let alone to do so publicly.

"It's fun being more than a friend," he murmured. "And I'm sorry I overstepped."

"You totally did!"

"I really am sorry if I made things difficult. But just so you know, you had it coming."

"What? How?" Anger flashed in her eyes again.

"Being awesome and so easy to brag about. I want to help you in any way I can."

Her shoulders relaxed and her gaze drifted through the window to where the kids were playing quietly with their new gifts.

Louis pulled her close again, giving her a long, sensual kiss. Then he released her, slid his beard back into place and left, hoping she was feeling at least a little bit charmed.

"Hey, y'all," Hannah said, smiling at her phone as her boys and ex-husband crowded around the screen on the other end of the video chat. She could catch glimpses of a statue of a man on a horse in the background, as well as a fountain and some trees. It looked like a wet and cool morning in Paris.

She was still feeling warm and fuzzy from Santa's visit at the day care earlier, and her head was drifting in the clouds over Saturday's date as well. Even though Louis had totally meddled. Again. Man, that had been so embarrassing and awful. And maybe she was too much of a softie to have forgiven him already. But before he'd left, one of the little ones had crawled into his lap and gone to sleep. Seeing him cuddling the small child while still playing with the others had done some irreversible ovary twitching and iceberg-in-her-heart thawing.

Before he'd left the day care she'd asked him if he might want kids.

His reply had been, "Might? No. I definitely do."

She'd never really considered having more children, or even remarrying, but in that moment her brain and hormones had gone wild, her imagination building a future that surely was never going to happen. Her and Louis with kids? Not so likely.

But she was starting to wish that it could happen.

"What did you do yesterday?" she asked her boys. It was late in Sweetheart Creek and early there. It felt so odd that they were ready to start their Tuesday while she was just putting an end to Monday. "Where are you?"

"We're outside! Gammy's still sleeping!" Thomas said, coming close enough to Calvin's phone that Hannah could see the shadowy circles of his nostrils.

"We're outside the hotel," Calvin stated.

"We ate ice cream!"

"Yesterday," Calvin said. "And we went to a museum."

"We ate ice cream *at* the museum," Wade declared.

Hannah's heart warmed at his enthusiasm. It looked like her sons were having a good adventure.

"I learned how to say thank-you in French," Thomas told her. He said something that sounded almost correct, while Calvin winced.

"We're working on our French," he explained.

"That's great."

As Wade and Thomas filled Hannah in on all they'd been up to, Calvin listened with a slightly odd look on his face.

"What's up?" she finally asked him, when the boys went digging through their bags to find the museum map. "How were your meetings?"

"Good. And I just wanted to say that I really

appreciate your support, Hannah. My mom didn't think you'd be up for me taking the kids on this exploratory trip, and it's been really great. We're bonding."

"I'm glad."

Thomas popped into view of the screen. "I wore out Gammy." He disappeared again, asking, "Where's the map?" His brother muttered something and the two began bickering.

Calvin mumbled something to the boys, then said to Hannah, "Anyway, I really appreciate that you're up for an international move, and how family-focused you are." His smile was warm and kind. She used to do anything for that smile.

Hannah eyed the notes she'd taken about the education classes and the costs of entering college in January. It was all very doable if she got a student loan, maybe a scholarship or two, as well as a few more hours at the day care. Assuming she didn't have the cost of moving to France—even though Calvin had said he'd cover most of it—and that she was accepted into the program.

"The meetings have been positive?" she asked.

"They have."

"When will you know if the project is the right fit?"

"Three to four weeks. It's all up in the air at

the moment. It could be longer. Maybe less." He gave a carefree laugh, obviously unbothered by the unknown and how it was leaving his entire family in limbo.

The winter semester at the college started in two weeks, but Hannah could take the first several classes toward her degree online, meaning she could be anywhere in the world. Although starting school while navigating a family move to a foreign country might be taxing.

"I heard a rumor about you," Calvin said, his lips quirked in a bemused expression.

"A rumor?" Hannah's mind immediately went to Louis. Had someone seen them kiss? The song "I Saw Mommy Kissing Santa Claus" started playing in her head.

"I'm not sure what to think of it." Calvin was watching her through the screen and she felt on the spot, like there was no way to hide or distract him from talking about the kiss.

"Well, life is unexpected and sometimes...things happen."

"Things happen?"

"Yeah. You know. Out of the blue."

"Out of the blue." His brow furrowed. "What *is* going on?"

"Louis Bellmore and I might be becoming

friends. He—" Hannah caught a glimpse of Thomas, who was reading his map, and realized she couldn't relay the story of Louis dressing up as Santa. Her little boy still held an impressive and tenuous belief in the existence of Santa Claus. Any day that bubble would burst, but she didn't want to be the one responsible.

Hannah opened her mouth to mention the plane ride instead, but that felt like the date it had become. Calvin had enjoyed the odd romantic outing himself in the past year, but Hannah felt the need to hold her relationship status close to her chest for some reason.

"I'll admit that for a moment I thought the rumors were true," he was saying.

Hannah felt her face heat up and she debated pretending there was a bad connection and hanging up.

"But seriously? That's as crazy as the one about you going back to school." He laughed. "You were so ready to get out of there when I finished my degree that you didn't even finish yours."

"Yeah. Crazy, isn't it?" Her face grew even hotter. She hated the Sweetheart Creek grapevine right now. Not only had her mom called her up, all confused about why she was insisting on becoming a career woman, but the rumor of her application had made it all the way to France in less than two days. How had she been so naive as to believe that she could wait to discuss this with Calvin in person?

It was like expecting her mother to understand. She was still unconvinced the divorce was necessary, and as for Hannah wanting her own financial independence, her mom had asked why she couldn't just "hold Calvin to his financial commitments" and be a stay-at-home mom like she'd always wanted.

But had she always wanted that? Yes, for a while. But she hadn't envisioned it being forever. And one day Calvin might have two families to support, or might be downsized at work. Hannah needed her own money. She needed to be able to move on.

"Wait. Is it true about school?" Calvin was staring at her, his face slightly pale in the December morning light.

"Um, maybe." She scrunched her nose, trying not to cringe. "I haven't totally decided. I've only just applied."

"I thought we were building toward a move to Paris." There was impatience and anger in his tone, to which Thomas was thankfully oblivious.

Wade, probably not so much. Being two years older he caught a lot of things Thomas didn't.

Her youngest held his map in front of the screen, blocking her view of Calvin. "There was a statue of a man with a sword and another one of a lady," Thomas announced. "Her one private was showing." He lowered the map to gesture to his chest, and beside him Wade giggled.

"Thomas, I need to chat with your dad."

Ignoring her request, he continued pointing out various things on the map as he chattered a mile a minute. "At the museum there were bathrooms everywhere. And ice cream and doughnuts, but Dad told me only one treat so I had an ice cream, but Gammy bought me a doughnut later because she didn't know. And there was a bench outside, with ducks on a pond. A lady let me feed them her pretzel."

"None of this is for certain yet, Calvin," Hannah said, after giving Thomas a quick hum of acknowledgment. "France and...everything." She waved a hand and slid her admission notes farther away.

"I thought we were on the same team. I thought we had a plan."

"We are! We do. I can take these courses anywhere." At least the first ones. "I could even study while sitting on that bench feeding the ducks a pretzel."

"A man said it was bad for the ducks, but I'd already given it to them," Thomas chimed in.

"An American education degree will be worthless in France. It's a completely different system." Calvin's voice was low and urgent. "You don't need a degree to work where you are, and we're both still paying off our student loans from before."

"I thought you'd like the idea of me expanding my financial independence. And *my* student loans are almost gone." That was one benefit of working so hard during school, as well as taking only a few classes.

"I take good care of you and the boys," he said. "I'm good about flexing my schedule or calling my mom to help us when Edith drops a shift in your lap, but that's for *work*."

"And I appreciate that."

"There's no need to change things. They're working fine."

Hannah sucked in a deep breath and held it to a count of five. She released it and sucked in a second one.

"I don't want to fight, Hannah." Calvin shook his head as though disappointed.

He wanted her to roll over. Withdraw from the program and lose the application fee, because it was inconvenient for him. Her choice could put them on separate pages in terms of their goals, and could even make him appear selfish if he moved them all to France when she wanted to go back to school.

In some ways Calvin and Louis weren't that different. They both wanted her to do things that suited their image of her. Louis wanted her to stretch more. Calvin less.

"What if something happens to your job?" Hannah asked. "Don't you want me to—"

"Where is all of this coming from?" When Hannah didn't reply, he said, "Is this about your neighbor? I heard he dressed up as Santa for you and that he wined and dined you with his big fancy NHL status."

"Louis is *Santa*? He's so cool!" Thomas's face popped into view of the camera. He gasped, his eyes widening. "Is his plane really a sleigh?"

"Santa's not real, dummy," Wade muttered.

"Wade," Hannah warned. "Louis was just helping out Santa. Santa's real busy this time of year. Louis is a hockey coach for the Dragons, the team Daisy-Mae, Athena and Violet work for."

"*Cool*. I bet he knows lots of players."

She nodded. "He does. I met some of them."

"Whoa!" Wade looked impressed.

"Can Louis take us to a hockey game?" Thomas asked, jostling his way into the camera's view again.

"Maybe. He took me to one."

Calvin's voice was low, almost a growl. "Since when do you like hockey?"

"Would he take me, too?" Wade asked hopefully.

"I thought this guy was your enemy, Hannah," Calvin said, angling the camera his way again. "And applying for school without discussing it with me—this is something that can impact all of us. We had an agreement about making big decisions that can affect our family, and you storming ahead isn't like you."

"I know. I'm sorry. I just want to be more independent. I want to be able to shoulder the responsibility that befalls me."

"Louis flies planes," Thomas told Wade. "I bet he could fly us home and then we could take our seat belts off whenever we wanted."

Calvin let out a big sigh. He slid back on the bench, the phone swaying in his grip. "We have to go." He ended the call before she could say goodbye to the boys.

Hannah blinked at her phone for a long minute before setting it down. Was this what Louis had been talking about? How everybody liked her being quiet and staying in her place?

Calvin obviously wasn't a fan of how she was potentially upending their lives, even if, overall, it would be better for everyone.

Then again, it was a rather sudden shift for her to go back to school, and she'd broken their agreement about discussing things like that ahead of time. She'd ambushed the poor man and she was certain that if she'd been the one to break the news to Calvin it would have gone much smoother. Instead, due to Louis's meddling, she'd sideswiped her ex, potentially making everything more difficult.

She dropped her head in her hands and sighed. All things being equal, it was going to be a very awkward Christmas.

9

Louis was exhausted. Away games, meetings, practices and the push to the Christmas holidays, as well as trying to spend time with Hannah, had him running non-stop. He had a new level of empathy for the players with families.

He hit his alarm and pulled himself out of bed, not bothering with a shirt to go with his loose running shorts. Two days until Christmas, and yet another away game tonight. He turned on the kitchen light, brewing his espresso extra strong.

He had time to woo Hannah a bit this morning if she was free.

His drink wasn't yet ready when he heard someone bang on his door, then try the knob.

Worried that Hannah might be having an emergency, he hurried over. Louis opened the door to find Hannah was beaming, her wavy hair a tousled mess.

"What's wrong?" No, wait. She was happy. Really happy.

She launched herself into his arms and his panic was gone in a flash. "Hey, good morning," he crooned against her neck. She smelled like chocolate chai and her soft chest melded to his own. She gave good hugs.

"I got in," she said breathlessly. "I checked my email this morning and I found it in my spam. I'm in!" She bounced out of his arms and started jumping in place as if she'd won the lottery.

"Congratulations!"

Her excitement faded abruptly as her eyes caught his bare chest. He swept a hand across it, resting the heel of his hand between his pectorals.

"You're so hot..." she murmured. She couldn't seem to lower her gaze, and he dropped his arm, letting her have a show. "I was waiting for your light to come on so I could tell you. I, um, I'm sorry...I..."

"Want me to put on a shirt?"

"Uh...."

He edged closer. "Or we could kiss."

Her eyes flew to his. He slid his hands down the arms of her long-sleeved shirt, then clasped her hands.

She smiled, leaned closer and accepted his offer, kissing him. She tasted the way she smelled, like chai. She was his new favorite smell and taste.

"When do you start school?"

"I—well, classes start in two weeks."

"Online or in person? Did you get a scholarship?"

She sucked in a deep breath and Louis could see the wave of panic hit her. She was in uncharted waters now.

"Hey, don't worry. It'll all fall into place."

"I don't even have a good laptop," she whispered.

"You can borrow mine. And that offer to take you to classes still stands."

"Thanks."

"You're worrying."

"I still don't know if Calvin is moving us all to France."

"Oh."

"Yeah. I mean, the cost of back and forth for the boys will break me."

"You want to stay in Sweetheart Creek?"

She was chewing her lip and didn't answer.

"Well, you could take online classes for now. Figure the rest out later?"

"What if we move and don't come back? What if he wants to stay there forever?"

"Hey, hey." Louis pulled her back into his arms. "This is your life, too, remember?"

"I don't want to go to France." She met his eyes with a desperation he wanted to erase for her. "I want to stay here. I want my adventures to be here."

Her eyes, if he wasn't delusional, were saying that she wanted to have those adventures here with *him*.

"Then make it happen, and let me know how I can help. I'd move mountains for you, Hannah Noelle."

Hannah really wished that whoever it was knocking on Louis's door would stop. She was having a lovely time kissing him, especially since he didn't seem to mind the way her hands kept exploring his bare torso.

She allowed him to extract himself from her embrace in order to answer the door. Her brows popped up when she saw it was MayBeth, the local real estate agent. Why was she here? Did Louis want to sell? Was Hannah's former Christmas wish coming true? Because at the moment she didn't really want him moving anywhere but back into her arms.

"Hi, Louis. Hannah. Merry Christmas."

"Merry Christmas," they chimed back.

"I thought I might find you here." MayBeth waved in the general direction of Hannah's house. "Sorry I got your dog all excited, knocking on your door just now."

"Oh. No problem. What's up?"

"I was just in the neighborhood and thought I'd drop off my card," she trilled.

"For me?" Hannah took the business card, feeling confused. Didn't she mean Louis? MayBeth had helped Hannah find her home, and they were already friends on every form of social media they both belonged to. She knew where to find MayBeth if she needed her.

Had Calvin made the decision to move to France? Was he already setting things in motion without talking to her? They were supposed to discuss things. And yeah, she'd broken that agreement by applying to school without telling him, but it wasn't like she'd packed her car and was already city-bound.

She focused on MayBeth, who was saying, "Spring is the optimal time for selling, but as soon as you're ready I can help you get your place on the market. We can work together on how to get the most money back in your pocket. I do have a family looking for a small starter home right now, though, and there's not a lot in this price range available. Do you want me to set something up? I'm sure you're eager to get moving and reclaim your down payment."

"Were you talking to Calvin?"

What time was it in Paris? He must have called MayBeth in the middle of the night to set things up.

"No, no. I heard y'all are moving. I thought maybe France, but your mom said back to the city." Her smile was bright. Innocent. "To go to school next month?" Her tone became uncertain as Hannah remained speechless. "I assumed you'll want to sell?"

"Thanks, MayBeth. Hannah will let you know if she needs anything." Louis edged between them, reaching for the door. MayBeth's eyes strayed down his naked chest, spending way too much time on their joyride for Hannah's comfort.

"I'm taking online courses. Maybe," she said through gritted teeth. "Things haven't been totally decided yet. Same with France."

"Oh. Well, I think it's great you're going back to school. You'll be a good teacher."

"Merry Christmas," Louis said, edging the door closed.

MayBeth began backing down the steps. "Merry Christmas!"

As soon as they were alone again, Hannah turned to Louis.

His smile was weak as he caught her expression.

"Thanks. A lot." She crumpled the business card and hunched her shoulders, struggling with her emotions.

"Uh, you're welcome?" He scratched the back of his head and gave her what was likely supposed to be a confused look.

"Why does the entire town think I'm moving to the city? And how did Calvin know I'd applied for school before I even had a chance to tell him?" She marched closer. "Why does my boss think I'm resigning?" Yeah, that had been a fun conversation. "Why did MayBeth just pop by to discuss putting my house on the market?"

The rumors and uncertainty stemming from

all of this was going to be hard on the boys. She needed to get the town under control before she picked them up from the airport tonight. They'd weathered the divorce well, but another move—possibly international—within a year, or their mom suddenly heading back to school and being less available? It might be too much uncertainty and change for two young boys.

What had she been thinking? She'd allowed herself to get pulled into some grand dream with no link to reality. That was the problem with Louis. He made her believe she could have a big life of fulfilled dreams without even noticing that it didn't fit with the things she truly valued, such as creating a stable home environment.

"This isn't the right time for this," she said. "None of it is."

"The whole town's proud of you," Louis replied gently. "They want to help you follow your dreams."

Hannah closed her eyes, trying to remain focused. She'd wanted support, and for the community to understand why she needed to do this. But now it felt like things were moving forward without her, and that was because of Louis. It felt as if she was undermining Calvin's desire to strike out fresh in Paris, as well as jamming a giant wedge between them and their ability to co-parent.

To make things worse, she must seem like a flake. First she was going to become a doctor, then she wasn't. She moved away to go to college, but didn't complete a diploma. She got married, then divorced. Moved back. Now she was moving to France or to the city or going to school? What *was* she doing?

"What if something goes wrong with getting this degree?" she asked, feeling a headache starting. "What if I can't hack it? What if I can't afford to finish? What if life happens?"

"You'll make it."

"I know I'll end up where I need to be, but you have to stop meddling, and let me be the driver. Stop trying to make my life into what you think it should be. I'm taking classes while living here in Sweetheart Creek. I'm not moving."

"I know."

"You told Edith I'm taking classes in the city and she was ready to advertise my job!"

"I didn't say you were moving."

"Then what, Louis? What? Everything you touch turns into a giant mess."

Her life had felt so simple a week ago. Smooth. Then she'd let him pull her into his world and now everything was turning into a disaster.

"Do you trust me?" Louis asked, an unfamiliar, impatient edge to his tone. "Like me? Want to spend time with me?"

"You don't seem capable of comprehending the no-meddling rule."

"Did it occur to you in the midst of this freak-out that maybe people just assumed you'd move away for school because it's what most people do, and it's what you did last time?"

"If you and I are going to humor the idea that we might have a chance, I need to be enough for you just the way I am. As I am at this very second in time. No changes. No big adventures. Just a single mom subsisting above the poverty level, happily living in a small town. Not some woman taking on the world and grand adventures, looking for a chance to break out into something huge. Me. Right here. Right now. As is."

Louis stepped back, crossing his strong arms, studying her.

"I'm a quiet people pleaser, Louis. Not everyone needs to be the CFO of a large company in order to be happy or feel satisfied with their life."

"I didn't say you did." His jaw was tight now, as was his voice.

"It's implied. I need to be with someone who doesn't push the whole town into...into whatever they're thinking and saying. I need someone who will support me if I change my mind and stay working in a day care. I don't need you to…" She had run out of words, and gestured helplessly.

"Meddle? Support? Help clear a path?"

"Yes! And create misunderstandings."

"So you'd rather do this alone, and not let others help you in case you fail—which you won't."

"Yes! No." She didn't know anymore. She only knew that Louis was causing things to spin out of control. "Returning to school is scary, and for the sake of my family, I need to keep everything as normal as possible."

"For Calvin."

"For my boys!"

"Why do you have to play small and he doesn't? Why can't you take online classes, when he's ready to move you all to a foreign country where they speak a language none of you do?"

Hannah froze, breathing hard. "You don't understand."

"You'd rather I help convince you that your

current life is just fine, and that there isn't more that you should want," Louis said. "That it's perfectly acceptable to be locked into a role where you pretend to be happy, struggling to subsist on handouts from your ex. Is that what you want? Is that what I'm supposed to shake my pom-poms over?"

"Leave Calvin out of this."

"I can't," Louis snapped. He paced a few steps, then finally met her eyes, a sad resolve settling in his. "He's a part of your life, and he's a part of what is holding you back from being you."

"I'm already me!"

"There's only one woman I want to be with, Hannah, and from what I'm hearing, she's too afraid to stand up and speak for what she wants."

"Louis. You're being melodramatic."

"No. I don't think I am." He stepped back. "I thought I could help you be brave enough to be the woman I see inside of you. But I guess I can't."

It was so late it was nearly Christmas Eve as Hannah stood in the arrivals area of the San Antonio airport, hands stuffed deep into her pockets while she waited for Calvin and the boys. To say she was still frustrated and upset about that morning's fight with Louis was an understatement.

Maybe he'd move away. Forever. An idea that hurt her heart.

Everything hurt.

Calvin, his mother and the boys had taken three different flights coming home from Paris, and Hannah had a strong feeling the kids would be exhausted, jet-lagged and basically as unhappy as a poked bear by the time they landed.

But once everyone was settled at home she could pretend that everything in her life was as it should be. They'd be back on schedule. Nobody was going anywhere. They would do their own thing tomorrow, then enjoy Christmas Day together. There would be no Louis pushing her, telling her to be someone else so he could love her.

She was back to being Hannah Murphy, no longer Kendrick, and ensconced in the quiet life she loved.

A life that now somehow felt as though something important was missing from it.

She scoffed at herself. All that was missing was the constant conflict that pushy Louis Bellmore brought to her world. And she did not miss that.

She'd pegged him early on as unable to go the distance, and yet she'd allowed her hopes to climb. But at least she hadn't dragged the boys into it. In the coming days they were going to be confused enough with everyone asking about her and school, as well as possibly moving overseas. The poor kids wouldn't know if their parents were coming or going, after she'd worked so hard all year to make sure they both felt stable.

And then in walks Louis for a few days, and everything becomes a mess.

Life was easier without him.

The opaque glass security doors opened and a large cluster of big men in nice suits exited, chatting, sports bags slung over their shoulders.

Hockey players. Hannah's heart skipped a beat. She recognized these guys. Louis's team was arriving home from their last away game before Christmas. She scanned their faces, suddenly wide-awake.

What was she doing? She was not looking for Louis. She was here for her sons, her ex, for Maureen. Family. *This* was her life. Not anything to do with that man.

She forced herself to read the signs near the baggage carousel. But after a few seconds she found herself scanning the crowd of hockey players again, just as her family finally came through the doors.

Calvin and Thomas looked grim and fed up with each other. Calvin had him by the hand, with Thomas trying to go limp on him, buckling his knees every time Calvin tried to make him stand. Wade looked like a zombie, but was at least still on his feet.

"Let's go," Calvin said to Thomas. "There's Mom!" He looked relieved, practically dragged their son across the floor and into her open arms. Thomas wound himself around her as Maureen, ignoring the whole scene, moved to the conveyor belt, where suitcases were starting to appear.

Thomas whined, "I'm tired."

"I know, sweetie." She kissed his cheek. "I missed you." She hugged him tightly, then pulled Wade to her side for an embrace. "How was the trip?" she asked her ex.

"Long. We're jet-lagged." Calvin pushed a hand through his hair. He stepped back, no doubt done with parenting exhausted boys.

Hannah whispered in Thomas's ear, "It's almost Christmas!"

He didn't respond. She wasn't sure if he was

asleep or just ignoring her. Although his weight hadn't suddenly amplified, which meant he was likely still conscious. She did some quick mental math. Paris was seven hours ahead, meaning they were about ready for breakfast.

"Are you hungry?"

Thomas shook his head.

"How about you, Wade?"

"I'd like some ice cream."

"Not sure that's going to happen," Hannah said. She tried to set Thomas down, but he refused to unhook his legs from around her. "Thomas, you're going to have to walk. You ate so much ice cream while you were away that I can barely lift you."

Maureen had found her suitcase and was already trucking ahead, toward the exit. With Thomas still in her arms, Hannah walked beside Calvin, who'd plucked up the rest of the bags.

"Things went okay?" She tipped her head toward his mom. Maureen and Calvin didn't always get along well, and right now the woman's mood suggested that she'd had it out with her son. Over what, Hannah didn't know, but the thought of gossip perked her up.

Calvin's jaw tightened, but he didn't offer anything other than "Things went fine."

He was still such a poor liar. He'd obviously done or said something his mother disagreed with. The good news for him was that she always forgave him almost immediately and would soon return to doting on him.

"Any word on a piano?" Hannah asked Calvin as they walked across the almost empty baggage corridor toward the doors.

"Hannah, I'm tired."

"I know. It's just that it's basically already Christmas Eve, and for the concert I—"

"It's Christmas. How will I get a piano?"

"I just thought maybe you'd had a line on something even though you were away."

"I texted you about it last week."

"I was just checking. In case... Did they make you a job offer?" She awkwardly shifted Thomas's weight. Her arms already felt exhausted and she didn't want to drop him.

"Mom, we're out this way," Calvin said tersely, directing her to the south as they caught up with her.

"Actually, I parked this way," Hannah said, nodding to the north. "Thomas? Can you walk? We have to take stairs down to the car and I don't want to fall."

He shook his head in the crook of her neck.

"Please." She lowered her arms, but he clung to her like a baby sloth.

If this was what it was going to be like after each trip to France, the situation would be torture for all of them.

"Come on, Thomas. You have to walk."

The weight in her arms was suddenly gone as Thomas was lifted from her.

"Here, I've got your little starfighter."

"Hi, Louis," Thomas gave him a shy, sleepy smile before dropping his head against his shoulder.

Louis caught Hannah's eyes over the boy's head. She looked tired, relieved and…not mad. He hadn't had time to question himself before honing in—meddling? He'd done what he told his players to do: when they saw a teammate in need, don't think, react.

And to him, even though Hannah was likely still mad and blaming him for all the scary potential changes in her life, she was a teammate.

"You don't have to carry him," she said quietly.

"I've got your back, Hannah." He held her eyes. "Always."

She nodded, her expression somber.

"What are you doing at the airport?" he asked Thomas. "Were you out on a special mission to fight drones?"

"You're silly."

"That's true."

"Were you at a hockey game?" Wade asked, falling into step beside him. He was eyeing Louis's suit and looking confused.

"You have dragons on your tie." Thomas giggled, his small fingers toying with it.

"Of course I do! That's my team." Louis glanced down at Wade. "I was coaching the guys. We wear suits to and from the arena. It's a thing." He leaned closer and confided, "I think they just like getting dressed up and showing off a little."

"Can I come to a game?" The note of yearning in the boy's polite request made Louis want to offer him a season's pass.

"If it's okay with your parents I can arrange a ticket for you. A good one close to the action."

"I can carry him." Calvin was at Louis's side, bags slung over his shoulder, arms out for his son.

"Nah, I've got him. You've got a big load there, Calvin."

Look at him being nice. He hoped Hannah was catching all of this. Particularly how he could fit into her life and be helpful, lighten the load and such. And do it all while *not* punching the lights out of the man holding her back. What could he say? He was the complete package.

"He's a big boy," Calvin said firmly, nodding at Thomas. "He can walk."

"I honestly don't mind. And I'm going this way," he lied. He had driven into the city for the flight instead of flying his Cessna, and his car was in the valet lot, in the opposite direction. In fact, if he'd realized Hannah was coming to the airport tonight he would have set her up with a spot there as well. And not just because it would have irked Calvin.

"How was the game?" Hannah asked. "I heard some of it on the radio on the way in."

"She doesn't even like hockey," Calvin said, jabbing a thumb in her direction.

"Calvin, take my bag," an older woman commanded. Calvin added it to his collection.

"Ma'am," Louis said, giving her a nod. "Louis Bellmore. And you must be Maureen?"

The woman's brows shot up and her eyes darted to Hannah.

"She told me you were in charge of her boys and she was mighty grateful you were taking the trip with them." He added for good measure, "Family's important."

"That it is." She lifted her chin, giving Calvin a pointed look, then said to Louis, "Lovely to meet you."

And before he realized what was happening, Thomas was being taken from his arms and set in Hannah's SUV, everyone saying goodbye.

Hannah leaned close, giving his arm a squeeze and him a breathless "Mighty grateful." Then she was pulling out into the night and Louis was wondering where exactly he stood with the woman of his dreams.

* * *

Once on the highway, Hannah asked her passengers how Disneyland Paris had been, assuming Calvin's earlier lack of reply about the job meant he didn't know and didn't want to speculate. She felt nervous, her hands damp on the wheel. Louis had swooped in. The boys adored him. She adored him. Calvin did not.

Louis was trouble. Nothing but trouble.

And she couldn't get him off her mind. She wanted the man in her life, but wasn't sure how she could swing it without everything in her life imploding. She wanted to fast-forward five years to more happy times, when things were settled—assuming they ever were. Would she be with Louis? Would she be alone? A teacher? A strong, independent woman?

She hoped at least some of the answers would be yes.

"The park was okay," Calvin answered. In the back seat, his mother was already snoring. The boys were also likely asleep, since they didn't pipe up.

"I want to register for two online classes," Hannah said. "They start the first week in January."

Calvin sighed. "Hannah, we were going to discuss this once I was home."

"Then now's the time, I guess. I might need to switch the odd child-care day with you during exams."

"I meant discuss this *before* you registered," he said, his tone impatient.

"I couldn't wait."

"Why? Why this sudden need? It's hardly the moment to overextend yourself financially or time-wise. How are we going to swing you going back to school in the city when we're raising our boys in two separate households hours away from there? And how are we going to swing school if we're all moving to France?"

"There is no 'we'," Hannah snapped. "And frankly, I'm not up to hearing about how my life is going to inconvenience yours. You should be happy I'm doing this! It'll give us both more freedom, independence, and will be better for the kids in the long run. You can't talk about Paris and not let me talk about school."

"It's different. I started that discussion almost two months ago."

"And I'm starting this discussion now. About what I want and need."

They drove the rest of the way to Sweetheart Creek in silence, Hannah's heart beating hard. Putting her foot down was exhilarating and terrifying, but it felt good. She didn't want to move away right now—to anywhere. But she did want to take classes.

Hannah dropped off Calvin's mom first, then pulled up outside his place. When she began unloading Wade, who was now bounding with energy, Calvin said, "I thought they could stay with you tonight."

It was after one in the morning and the boys were gearing up like it was 8:00 a.m.—which it was in Paris. That meant they were ready to go at the day full throttle, and she hadn't yet fallen asleep.

"Maybe the three of you should stay here, take a nap this afternoon, then get up for the concert. Work through your jet lag together, since you'll all be on the same schedule." She coaxed Thomas out of the car and put his hand in Calvin's.

Wade was sprawled on the lawn, staring up at the night sky. "I can see stars!" he said with glee. "I'm up way past my bedtime!"

Calvin was staring at Hannah, looking dazed. "But I really need some rest."

"I know. So do they. So do I." Hannah backed away, her heart breaking at giving up the boys on what should be her day with them. But she could see it in her mind as clearly as if it was happening. Calvin would go take care of himself, and she'd be up all night with two boys whose bodies thought it was morning. She'd exhaust herself before the concert and Christmas, moving through both special occasions like a zombie so Calvin could recover faster, when it had been his choice to put himself through the jet lag in the first place. Then he'd boast about how it was nothing to take their kids back and forth through several time zones.

Hannah crouched down to where Wade was

still on the grass. "I'm going to go home and sleep, since it's my bedtime. You can come over to our house in the morning, okay?"

"Okay."

"Love you."

He leaped into her arms, giving her a big hug. "I love you, Mom."

She staggered under the unexpected weight of her eldest, then glanced at Thomas, still standing with Calvin. It was as if her boys had done a body switch during the trip and drive. Wade had grudgingly given her a hug when he'd left for the airport, and now here he was… She buried her nose in his hair, making a point not to overstay this unexpected embrace in case it caused him to not want more in the future.

She tickled Thomas's chin as she passed him. "Love you, kiddo. See y'all tomorrow."

Calvin gaped at her as she got back into the car, hurrying before she changed her mind. As she started the engine, her legs were trembling from the way she'd finally stood up for herself, and for what she wanted. What she needed.

A part of her wished Louis had been there to see it.

10

It was Christmas Eve and Louis watched Hannah, who was waiting to play the piano for the children of Sweetheart Creek during the community Christmas concert. She looked nervous, unable to stay still, twisting a song book into a tube before finally dropping it onto the piano bench. Her soft curls brushing the shoulders of her red Christmas sweater, which showed Mrs. Claus surrounded by gingerbread men. Hannah was wearing a headband with reindeer antlers, and he was pretty sure her earrings were holiday themed as well.

Louis looked down at his own green sweater, one with Santa drinking a beer. He hoped she noticed the effort he'd made, because in his world paying money for an ugly Christmas sweater (yuck), one he'd probably never wear again, was a *thing*. A thing worth noticing.

Folding chairs had been set out in the old barn, and several live trees from Cassandra's sale scented the space with pine. It felt like Christmas in here as bodies warmed the room, colored lights twinkled merrily in the rafters above, and the fir trees in each corner filled the room with their fresh scent. There was a short one with red and green lights by the low stage and the ancient piano. At six that morning he'd nearly knocked it over several times as he and his friend Ryan Wylder toiled over replacing the instrument's dead key.

The wonky old piano sounded better. Not great, but better. In his imagination, when Hannah played it tonight, it would sound cute, somehow adding to the enthusiasm of the excited children as they sang.

The program began, and behind the MC, Louis spied Hannah helping the first singer onto the stage, bending low to talk to her. Hannah was all smiles, her earlier nerves apparently forgotten as she put the child at ease.

The barn was packed and Louis leaned against the back wall like he had at age seventeen, giving up his seat so Mrs. Fisher could sit along the aisle where her husband was parked in his motorized scooter. He'd decked it out like it was a Harley, complete with a license plate that said BAD ONE, fancy silver tire rims with flames painted around them, and more.

Louis yawned, the warmth of the room and his lack of sleep over the past week getting to him. He eyed the snack table set near the entrance. Under the festive drop cloth were cookies, hot chocolate and best of all, coffee. He sure could go for a cup.

Up front, Hannah was seated on the piano bench, stroking the silent keys with reverence, centering and preparing herself. After fixing the broken one he'd rubbed polish onto the old, lacquered cabinet. He'd thought of Hannah the whole time, wondering how she'd react to the repaired instrument, what she thought about him swooping in to carry Thomas last night. Louis figured from now on the scent of old wood and fresh polish would make him think of her.

He'd even taken time to polish the brass pedals, giving them a glorious shine. He'd poured some serious love into the instrument and Ryan had simply given him a knowing smile and headed home to do his chores once his part of the job was done.

Hannah looked over her shoulder before she hit a key, her eyes locking on his. Louis gave a slow nod of acknowledgment and kept his hands in his jeans pockets, waiting, watching, his nervousness building.

She mouthed a *"thank you"* and turned back to the piano. Out came the first few bars of "Rudolph the Red-Nosed Reindeer." The plinking of the keys was jovial and upbeat, and the little girl began belting out the lyrics. The piano sounded less rich than a properly tuned one might, but people were smiling and he figured that was good.

The child finished her song and curtsied to the crowd, which applauded even louder. She shot them a smile missing her front top teeth.

Louis watched Hannah play the next carol. In between singers she spun on her bench, searching the audience. When she spotted her boys she wiggled her fingers, Thomas's small head popped up and his arm stretched into the air as he waved at her. His enthusiasm had to make her feel special.

There was an empty seat beside Calvin and the boys, and Louis wondered if it was reserved for Hannah, even though she was on stage. And if so, had it been saved by Calvin or the children?

Would there be a Christmas miracle next year that caused her reserved seat to be beside Louis instead?

From what Louis had heard while picking up a coffee at the Longhorn Diner after working on the piano, nobody would be in France next Christmas. He'd heard Daisy-Mae and Mrs. Fisher saying that Hannah had put her foot down, but then Ryan had also mentioned something about Calvin not being impressed with the agency that was recruiting him. Louis didn't much care which story was true as long as Hannah stayed in Sweetheart Creek, but he secretly hoped it was the former reason.

The next performer was ready and Hannah began working that musical magic that always enthralled him and had brought him to music as well. Her fingers began to dance, the song so familiar that she kept her eyes on the child singing rather than the keys.

Hannah's boys performed the last song a half hour later, decked out in fake Santa beards as they sang "Up on the Housetop." When she played "Here Comes Santa Claus," the entire audience joined in, eyes toward the doors where Santa was due to come through. Which he did with a loud "Ho, ho, ho."

Santa settled himself on the stage and began distributing gifts from his sack. Louis planned to leave, but got distracted by Hannah's genuine happiness as she helped Santa and the kids.

Then the concert was over and adults and kids alike swarmed the snack table, scrambling to get their hands on Hannah's chocolate cherry cookies. Louis could see Calvin watching him with an assessing gaze that he figured could go either way, good or bad.

By now Calvin had likely heard how he'd convinced her to apply to school as well as to say no to France—he'd take credit for that. Top that off with how he'd given her the VIP hockey treatment in what the press were speculating was an official date, as well as carrying Calvin's son last night and, well, Louis figured the man might need a little space.

* * *

Hannah scanned the community barn for familiar faces. Specifically, Louis's. She wanted to thank him for the effort he'd put into the old piano. He'd brought out the beauty in the instrument's wood grains, transforming its battered old appearance and flaws into something to admire. Even the silent key had rung true tonight, having found its voice in a gentle repair.

Louis had seen this piano's potential, just like he'd seen her own.

But she couldn't find him. Earlier he'd been standing against the wall, but now he was gone, and Calvin was approaching, along with her parents. Hannah's mom and dad gave her hugs and well wishes before heading out into the dark night, with promises of seeing her tomorrow for Christmas dinner.

Thomas launched into her, and she ruffled his hair, wishing it was her night to have him. It felt as though Calvin had had the boys for so long with the trip, and now a bonus day of jet lag recovery. And while she knew it would all even out in the long run, she still felt as though she was losing out.

"You played well," Calvin said. His posture was slightly awkward as they stepped to the side to let people flow past the cookie table. "Did he get you a new piano?"

"Who?" she asked innocently.

"You know."

"Louis?"

He gave a small nod, glancing cautiously in the boys' direction as though fearing they might burst into happy song at hearing the man's name.

"He just brought out the best in this one." Hannah snagged a gingerbread man from the table, breaking its head off before realizing she wasn't actually hungry.

Calvin ran his fingers through his hair, his gaze on Hannah's boots. When he looked up, he let out the breath he'd been holding. "I think he's also brought out the best in some other things, too."

Hannah's breath froze in her chest and she tried to stop her eyes from opening so wide."What do you mean?" she asked, feigning casualness.

Calvin took her by the elbow and steered her farther from the snack table so they'd have more privacy. The boys had found the hot chocolate and Wade was patiently helping Thomas in a way he wouldn't have a week ago. The trip had been good for them, and it was so nice to see them exhibiting independence, as well as how their relationship as brothers had grown.

Maybe change wasn't something to be afraid of on their behalf. Maybe it was something they all needed.

"You seem different," Calvin said.

"I'm not."

"A few weeks ago you wouldn't have decided to go back to school." Hannah inhaled sharply, and Calvin added quickly, "It's good. I like it. And you're right to want more for yourself. I'll help you in any way I can, and I'm sorry I wasn't more supportive about it earlier."

"I should have brought it forward for discussion first."

"No, I have no business. This is your decision."

"It'll impact all of us."

"That still doesn't make it my business or my decision to make for you. I trust that you didn't make this choice lightly, and I know you've considered all the angles. I hope you'll ask for the help you need, when you need it. I know you want more independence, and I admire and respect that. But that doesn't mean I get to renege on my obligations."

Obligations. Somehow, somewhere along the line that was what she'd become to him. It was an unfortunate word choice, but she understood the intended sentiment. He was here and had her back, just like she'd had his during their school years. It wasn't his fault—or hers—that their love hadn't been enough to keep their marriage intact. But they were still in this together, as parents.

"You're a good man," she whispered, barely trusting her voice.

"I could be better."

"We could all be better."

"I said no to France," Calvin murmured, as they waved to Violet and Cassandra. Both of them were fussing over Dusty, whose face was covered in chocolate.

"What? Why?"

"It was asking too much."

"The job?"

"No, moving overseas. It was too much to ask of all of us." He glanced toward his mom, who was chatting with Mrs. Fisher. "I was being selfish."

The tension that had been weaving through Hannah over the past few days tightened, then suddenly unspooled as she realized France was never going to happen.

She felt lighter, free. Her family was staying put. The only disruption in the New Year would be her spending time with her nose buried in textbooks. And she was fairly certain they could all handle that.

"Thank you." She stepped closer to Calvin,

giving him a hug that felt familiar but strangely devoid of love. They were partners raising their children and nothing more. And he was supporting her so she could finally be truly free. Free to be herself. Free to follow her dreams and her heart. She slipped from his embrace and gently touched his cheek. "Thank you. Really."

"You'll always have a special place in my heart."

She laughed, knowing it would never be in a romantic sense, and for the first time it truly and honestly felt like that was okay. That *she* would be okay.

The barn was emptying quickly and they shifted closer to the door, calling to the boys. As they did, a strange mix of sadness and joy filled Hannah. Tonight felt like a final goodbye. An ending to a large part of the life she'd always imagined with Calvin.

But on the horizon there was the unknown, the opportunity to get to know herself better, thanks to the meddlesome ways of a man named Louis. A man she felt she owed an apology to.

She missed him. He was trying, just like she was. The man was far from perfect, but so was she. But when they were together it felt as though they were both a little closer to it.

"You'll tell me if you need anything for school?" Calvin asked, handing Hannah her jacket from the coatrack.

"I'll need extra child care from time to time," she told him, zipping it up as she waited for Maria Wylder and her boyfriend, Clint Walker, to exit first.

Calvin nodded, a slight smile haunting his lips. "A few weeks ago you wouldn't have asked."

"I'm the same as I was!" she insisted.

"No. This is good." There was affection and approval in his gaze, and it felt weird. She hadn't seen that from him, or really anyone other than Louis, in a very long time, and it felt out of place. "I like that you're standing up for what you need, even if it means you're going to be busting my chops a lot more." He winked before she could get upset. At the threshold, he reached out to touch her sleeve again, saying softly, "It looks good on you."

"Thank you."

He tipped his head toward the grassy parking lot surrounding the old barn, and Hannah scanned the people mingling in the glow cast by the outdoor lights. Louis was standing, waiting, hands in his jeans pockets. He was handsome, calm and somehow sure of himself despite their tough words yesterday morning. The idea that he might be waiting for her even though she wasn't woman enough for him made Hannah's heart give one of those skips that would alarm a cardiologist.

"I don't know what happened that made you two friends, but I think it's good." There was that flicker of a smile from Calvin again. "Go say hi." He gave her a nudge.

"We're fighting," she said, suddenly uncertain. What if she and Louis made up, dated, and then she ended up single and alone again like she had with Calvin?

Her ex-husband chuckled. "If the two of you ever stop fighting, that's when everyone needs to worry." He smiled, and suddenly he was that teenage boy she'd once wanted to win over. The boy she'd believed would always be on her side.

And here he was, back again, but as a friend this time. It was nice to have him in her corner.

Louis straightened as Calvin left the barn, rounding up the boys after he said goodbye to Hannah. They'd been inside a long time. Louis had planned to leave, but then decided to wait for her.

Calvin, as he passed, gave him a nod without a hint of resentment or animosity. Louis returned it, curious as to what had changed in the man. Was it simply the spirit of the season? A visit from the ghost of Christmas past, who'd told him to let his ex go so she could live a full life?

Louis put out a hand for the boys to high-five on their way by. "Hey, little man."

Thomas jumped, slapping Louis's palm with his own. "Hey, big man!"

Wade gave a nod, acting cool, but gave him a subtle fist bump.

Hannah stopped in front of Louis as her family continued on. "Merry Christmas."

"Was the piano okay?"

"Someone brought out the best in it." She'd zipped a tendril of her brown curls into the collar of her jacket and Louis longed to cozy up to her and free the strands. Instead he practiced patience, letting Hannah slowly come to the conclusion he'd already jumped to, that they were meant to be together.

Man, it was difficult to be patient, though. While he leaped into things with only his intuition and a gut feeling as his wingman, she considered every angle before taking action. It was one of the reasons Louis loved her, even though it drove him a little crazy.

Then again, she did a good job of jumping in where fighting him was concerned. Unfortunately for his less patient side, it sure seemed to slow their progress in the relationship department.

“I was ready to scrap the piano, but I was wrong.” She was watching him, her cheeks rosy, a hint of fear in her eyes. Fear of rejection? Of an I-told-you-so?

“That’s funny.”

She crossed her arms in that classic Hannah’s-annoyed posture. “What is?”

“I was wrong, too.”

She tipped back in surprise, one hand coming up to her chest as though trying to steady her heart. “You were?”

Louis shifted closer. “I was wrong about you.”

“What?” She sounded breathless.

“I judged you for caring about others. And you’re right. I saw my mother in you. You share a lot of her traits. Admirable traits, such as how tuned in you are with your values, and how you’ll set everything aside for your family. I didn’t see that quality for what it truly was, and I feared that you were getting the raw end of a bargain, that you were being…" The word *complaisant* was on the tip of his tongue. "That you weren't putting what *you* wanted before others. I was wrong, and I'm sorry."

"Oh."

"I talked to my dad earlier." Louis let out a breath, and said quickly, "My mom was sick before she left her job at Cohen's. She quit and stayed home so she could be with us, because she knew her days were numbered. She wanted to spend her best, last days with us." He swallowed hard, his throat tightening.

"Oh, Louis." Hannah moved to his side, giving his arm a squeeze.

He still couldn't quite wrap his head around the way he'd so steadfastly believed that his mom's illness had manifested from her giving up her dreams, and that Hannah was paddling the same boat. He'd erroneously thought that the two women were almost the same, and that he was somehow saving Hannah by pushing her so hard.

Louis pushed his hands deep into his coat pockets, his chest expanding. "I'm really sorry I took it out on you."

"Don't be. You helped shape me into who I am today, and I like who I am."

"So do I." His throat was tightening up again, but he worked his way past it. "I care about you, Hannah."

"I care about you, too." The warmth in her smile and tone felt good.

"That wasn't what I was hoping to hear."

Her smile fell, but while he expected her old fighting stance to make an appearance again, it didn't.

"Maybe I should say it first." His fingers found hers, entwining their hands together. "I love you, Hannah. I want nothing but the best for you, and I hope somehow, even though I'm just some guy who annoys you, that you'll find room for me in your life."

She blinked as if she'd been shocked. Louis wasn't certain she was even breathing. He was starting to grow concerned that he'd truly broken her this time when she threw her arms around him, nestled her face against his neck and breathed him in.

Louis savored the way she felt in his arms, wrapped in his embrace.

He knew it was a lot to ask that she return his feelings, especially in the wake of her divorce, with their history, and given their up-and-down week. But he'd said it. Put it out there. The rest was up to her, plus fate, destiny, or whatever lucky being had brought her back into his life.

"Does this hug mean I can stick around and continue to be a meddling pain in your butt?" he whispered against her neck. He wanted to kiss his way up to her lips, tangle his hands in her hair and never come up for air.

Air was for sissies who'd never met a woman like Hannah.

She slid out of his arms and stood in front of him, hands on her hips. "I thought you were going to try and reform your awful, meddlesome, argumentative ways?"

"Nope." He gave her a big grin to hide his nervousness. "You have to love me just the way I am, because most of the time I'm right."

"Good."

"What?"

"Don't change a single thing about your meddlesome, bratty self." She waggled a finger at him, her eyes twinkling, and man, he wanted to kiss her.

Instead he released the laugh that had built up in his chest, his heart lifting, his tension ebbing. He ran the pad of his index finger down her nose, then gave it a light tap before slipping one hand to her hip and the other against her neck, his thumb caressing her jaw. "And why should I stay like this and not reform?"

She narrowed her eyes as though he was laying a trap, her body leaning into his. "Because I love you, you big, bossy know-it-all. You were right about my life."

She said something else but his ears had stopped working.

She loved him.

Hannah Murphy loved him.

She let out a quick, loud sigh as though already regretting what she was saying. It didn't matter. His brain was already doing celebratory laps around his skull, chanting that she loved him. That was all he ever needed to hear.

"You pushed me to start making changes," she said with a huff, and he focused on her again. "They're small and potentially disruptive, but I'm fairly sure they'll pay off." She finished huffing and met his eyes. "And I hope that you'll be here to watch them happen."

"I will," he said, pulling her tight against him with both arms. "Always. No other place I'd rather be."

She leaned back, splaying her palms against his chest. He reminded himself to be patient. That Hannah made decisions a lot slower than he did.

But when she made them, he knew she'd be locked in.

"You also need to know that I'm not some big adventure," she said, her tone slightly scolding. "I like living here, and I like being a mom and having things in my life just so."

"You don't know me very well, do you?"

"Um, you spend more time in the air in a week than most people do in a lifetime."

"Hannah, you're all the adventure I need. Plus you're more adventure than you realize."

"No, I'm not."

"You keep me on my toes *all* the *time*."

She laughed, then tipped her head to the side, giving him a look best described as Mom-is-amused-but-trying-to-act-unimpressed. She was adorable.

"Sometimes, Hannah," he said in a confiding tone, "a man roams the earth and does crazy things like jumping out of planes because there is no one waiting for him at home. There's no one to hold his hand and snuggle against him while watching some cheesy romantic flick. There's no one lighting up when he walks in the door. No one to share his secrets and dreams with. And so he keeps looking. Keeps going on these adventures in hopes of chasing away the emptiness inside. Taking risks and trying to find a way to light up that dark void."

He gathered her hands from his chest and cupped them between his own, whispering, "Hannah Murphy, you chase away my emptiness. You challenge me to think differently, and you are all the adventure a man like me will ever need."

Her eyes grew damp and Louis's heart felt about eight million times too large for his body. It was the most brilliant, wonderful feeling in the world.

"I don't believe you," she muttered huskily.

"Believe me. Because I'm here to stay."

"Why, though?" She seemed thoroughly baffled, as if blind to the power she held over him.

"Because I love you."

She stared at him for a long moment, as though searching for more of an explanation. That would come in time, because some things you simply couldn't put into words. They had to be experienced.

She sighed softly and melted into his arms again. "I love you, too, Louis Pain-in-the-Butt-in-a-Good-Way Bellmore."

They met each other's eyes and chuckled at the absurdity of it all. Enemies to lovers. The chuckles turned to giggles, then outright laughter. Before long they were helpless with mirth, hardly able to breathe. Hannah looked at him and pointed, and their laughter started up all over again.

"Can I lock up? Or do you two need me to call a mental hospital?" Athena asked, popping her head out of the barn and giving them a skeptical look.

They burst out laughing again and Louis shook his head, unable to answer. The door closed.

"Who would ever have thought?" Hannah said at last, her laughter ebbing. She snuggled back into his arms where she belonged.

"I kind of had a suspicion." And before she could ask him when it had all started, he kissed her, hoping she'd forget about everything but the man standing in the cold, keeping her warm, safe and loved.

* * *

Hannah parked her car in her driveway, then met Louis, who had followed her home from the concert, on the lawn in front of her house.

His was the only one on the street that didn't

have Christmas lights, and as she wrapped her arm around his waist, she asked, "Think we'll ever get you in the spirit of the holiday?"

He chuckled. "This one's looking up, which will surely help the effort." He leaned down and kissed her. The surety of his arms around her were all she needed for a Christmas gift.

As they broke the kiss, she said, "I saw that you're wearing a Christmas sweater." She frowned at him in question.

"That was for you."

"For me?"

"Yeah."

"Hmm. So next year, lights on your house?"

"I was thinking I might be living somewhere else by then."

"You're moving?" She leaned back from him, her jaw dropping.

"Oh," he said, feigning innocence, "I thought you'd invited me to come live with you."

She laughed. "Louis!"

"What?"

"Slow down."

"Slowpoke."

"Living next door to each other is basically living together."

He snugged her tight. "Not even close, so don't you dare try to argue that it is."

She laughed, still marveling that this man loved her. They were such opposites, and yet somehow it worked. "You know everyone is being pretty incredible about me going back to school. Calvin's come around, and my friends have already offered to babysit for me."

"Yeah? I'm glad."

"No I-told-you-so?" she asked.

"Nope. I'm glad I was right."

"Cocky. You're cocky."

He smiled. "Confident."

"Yeah, me too." She was confident that things were going to work out. And it was all because of this man holding her in his arms.

"I'm often right, you know," Louis murmured. He leaned in to kiss her cheek. "Merry Christmas."

Hannah put one hand on her hip and gave him a look, then tapped her lips with the other. "Put it here, mister."

He complied, and she slipped her arms around his neck, bringing him in for a wonderful Christmas Eve kiss. She didn't want him to go home. She didn't want this evening to end. Tomorrow was going to be a zoo, with Calvin and the boys coming over at the crack of dawn, and the day would go late with traditions, family events and more. But right now she had Louis all to herself with no distractions.

Realizing she had the perfect excuse to spend more time with him, she broke the kiss and said, "I have a gift for you."

"More kisses?" He angled in for another, which she granted.

"Not a kiss," she said softly, her arms still around his neck.

"Another pocket knife?"

She gave him a sharp look. "What?"

"The first one is still going strong."

She'd noticed that he still had it and used it, but she hadn't realized he'd known that high school secret Santa gift was from her.

He smiled, that same generous, warm one that made her feel like she'd found her home. "It's something I've always treasured. Thank you. I've always wondered, though. Why give me such a nice gift when I was a thorn in your side?"

"It just felt right."

They stared at each other for a long moment. There was still so much to discover about this man, Hannah realized. So much she'd incorrectly assumed, and needed to alter. She had a hunch he felt the same way about her.

"What's your gift?" he asked.

"Oh! Right. It's inside." She led him into the house and hurried to her tree. Presents for the boys spilled out from under it and she grabbed the emergency gift she'd wrapped in case she needed to reciprocate with an unexpected offering. Holding the box of baking, and spying the unopened gift he'd given her at the day care while playing Santa, Hannah wondered why she hadn't considered getting something special for Louis this year. Was it all the fighting? The mounds of denial she'd steeped herself in when it came to how attracted she was to him?

He'd slipped off his boots to follow her into the living room, and she handed him the wrapped box of cookies. "It's not much."

He took it, looking at her for a long moment. "How do I deserve you?"

She laughed and gestured to the gift. "Open it, and you'll rethink that statement."

He unwrapped the box, then smiled. "I told my dad about these. I look forward to returning the container and using it as an excuse to come over to kiss you good-night tomorrow."

"Well, I'd better bake more cookies then, because I expect that every night. You know, with you living so close and all." She raised her brows mockingly. "Practically *living* together."

He let out a short burst of laughter, and hefted the cookies. "As for the size of gift, you should know, based on your Santa-Louis present, that I appreciate ones from the heart."

"I haven't opened it yet!" Hannah zipped back to the tree. "I wanted to wait until you were with me, and then I was too mad."

They took a seat beside each other on the couch, and as Hannah peeled off the wrapping paper, Louis's leg began to jiggle.

She paused and looked at him. "It's not a ring, is it?"

He paled and shook his head.

His leg-jiggling continued.

Before she could lift the lid on the box, he placed a hand over it. "This is—I don't mean for this to start a fight. I mean this gift in a good way. Supportive."

Oh, boy.

Holding her breath, Hannah opened the box. Inside was a gift card to the college's bookstore, a bag of chocolate-cherry-flavored coffee labeled for all-nighters, pens, a babysitting coupon from him, as well as an envelope with Hannah's name written in his tight scrawl. It held a coupon for a plane ride whenever she needed perspective.

Hannah's eyes grew damp at his thoughtfulness, his generosity, and the way she felt so supported.

She was glad she hadn't opened the gift days ago, because she might not have seen it for what it truly was. A friend in her corner. A friend who loved her and wanted the best in life for her.

No, scratch that. A more-than friend. A boyfriend.

Taking a deep breath, Hannah wrapped him in her arms and kissed him slowly.

For all his flaws, Louis was the right man for her, and she knew she would never want anyone else. And she couldn't wait to explore all the ways that made him the man she loved.

"I think I'm going to like the fact that you moved in next door." She waved the babysitting coupon and he laughed.

His expression became somber. "Are you going to tell the boys we're dating?"

"Is that what we're doing?"

"Yes."

"Good, because I plan on introducing myself to everyone as your girlfriend. And, yes, I'll tell them tomorrow."

Louis held her tighter so he could kiss her slowly.

There were a lot of things to look forward to when it came to being Louis Bellmore's girlfriend.

EPILOGUE

New Year's Eve

Hannah hooked her arm through Cassandra's, weaving her way among the few remaining spectators as the arena emptied. They followed Rylnn, Landon's four-year-old daughter, and Hannah's boys down the wide hallway toward the players' area.

"So? You and Landon, huh?" she asked Cass, low enough that the kids wouldn't overhear. "When will we see a ring on your finger?"

The arena had gone wild with an on-ice proposal between a player and a staff member, and

Hannah, head over heels in love with Louis, had nothing but marriage on her mind at the moment.

She still couldn't believe she was in love with the man who'd been such a thorn in her side for so many years. How had she ever been so blind to the kind of guy he really was?

During the night's home game, watching from the sky box, she'd felt her heart skip whenever she'd seen him on the large screen above the ice. That was her boyfriend, running a team of professional athletes. He was in charge, full of thought and strategy.

So sexy, too. She couldn't wait until he was done with his post-game meetings with the team and press so she could wrap her arms around him, smother him in kisses, and tell him how hot and sexy he was.

Cassandra was quiet and Hannah paused, pulling her aside to get a better look at her. "What? What's wrong?"

Her friend's mouth flickered, giving a brief smile as she started moving again. "Nothing's wrong."

"Is it Dusty?"

No, his surgery had gone well, and Cassandra was staying at Landon's city apartment and spending her days with her son until he was released, hopefully sometime next week. Hannah had needed to plead as well as twist Cass's arm to get her to come to tonight's home game.

"He's doing really well."

"Is it about Landon paying for it all? Did you fight?" Something was off. Something big.

"We're doing okay, but we're not on the marriage path," Cass said carefully.

Her friend had been through a bad marriage and rough divorce. Deep down was she actually cautious, despite her public devil-may-care mischievous side?

"Is it Landon? Does he not want marriage?"

The seemingly flawless way Cass and Landon had blended their families was like a fantasy. The kids loved hanging out with each other and they acted like a big family. Why not get married?

"Wait." Hannah stopped short. "Is it you? Are you not in love with him?"

"Love isn't the problem," she said, becoming more agitated.

"I don't get it."

Cass sighed, stopped moving, looked both ways for eavesdroppers, then lowered her voice and said, "Our relationship is…one of convenience."

Convenience? Cass and Landon? It all looked so real from the outside.

"You've given up on love?" Hannah asked, aware too late that she'd said it loud enough that a few heads turned their way. She gave a fake laugh as though they were joking, and nudged Cass before scurrying on down the hallway, catching up with the kids. "But I don't understand. You two look like you're in love."

"One of us is, but we have a deal. And it doesn't include love."

WOULD YOU LIKE A BONUS SCENE?

Available for a limited time...as an extra treat—because Santa says you've been good this year! There's an extra little scene for readers that goes beyond this book with Hannah and Louis. It's a sweet little scene with them and the boys. To read it, simply go to www.jeanoram.com/CCCbonus for your Chocolate Cherry Cabin bonus scene!

HOCKEY SWEETHEARTS: HAVE YOU READ THEM ALL?

The Cupcake Cottage

Peach Blossom Hollow

Chocolate Cherry Cabin

The Peppermint Lodge

Sugar Cookie Country House

The Huckleberry Bookshop

The Gingerbread Cafe

There are two more series set in Sweetheart Creek!

The Cowboys of Sweetheart Creek, Texas

The Cowboy's Stolen Heart (Levi)

The Cowboy's Secret Wish (Myles)

The Cowboy's Second Chance (Ryan)

The Cowboy's Sweet Elopement (Brant)

The Cowboy's Surprise Return (Cole)

Indigo Bay

Sweet Matchmaker (Ginger and Logan)

Sweet Holiday Surprise (Cash & Alexa)

Sweet Forgiveness (Ashton & Zoe)

Sweet Troublemaker (Nick & Polly)

Sweet Joymaker (Maria & Clint)

MORE SMALL TOWN ROMANCES BY JEAN ORAM...

Veils and Vows

The Promise (Book 0: Devon & Olivia)

The Surprise Wedding (Book 1: Devon & Olivia)

A Pinch of Commitment (Book 2: Ethan & Lily)

The Wedding Plan (Book 3: Luke & Emma)

Accidentally Married (Book 4: Burke & Jill)

The Marriage Pledge (Book 5: Moe & Amy)

Mail Order Soulmate (Book 6: Zach & Catherine)

Blueberry Springs

Whiskey and Gumdrops (Mandy & Frankie)

Rum and Raindrops (Jen & Rob)

Eggnog and Candy Canes (Katie & Nash)

Sweet Treats (3 short stories—Mandy, Amber, & Nicola)

Vodka and Chocolate Drops (Amber & Scott)

Tequila and Candy Drops (Nicola & Todd)

Champagne and Lemon Drops (Beth & Oz)

ACKNOWLEDGMENTS

A special thank you goes to Nate for naming Leo for me. Also for coming up with the meet cute for this story. He suggested the scene where Leo and Violet met, but wasn't super impressed with my version of it. I guess it didn't match up with what he had envisioned in his imagination. He did say I could use his idea including Leo saying, "You have a pretty face."

For those who found the wooing tips that Violet teaches Leo intriguing, these are based off of the love languages that are described much more fully in Gary Chapman's book *The Five Love Languages*.

Thanks to my editor Margaret, my beta reader team, my error team and my Jeansters.

ABOUT THE AUTHOR

Jean Oram is a *New York Times* and *USA Today* bestselling romance author. Inspiration for her small town series came from her own upbringing on the Canadian prairies. Although, so far, none of her characters have grown up in an old schoolhouse or worked on a bee farm. Jean still lives on the prairie with her husband, two kids, and big shaggy dog where she can be found out playing in the snow or hiking.

Become an Official Fan:
www.facebook.com/groups/jeanoramfans

Newsletter: www.jeanoram.com/signup
Website & blog: www.jeanoram.com

Find a complete, up-to-date book list at:
www.jeanoram.com/books

Printed in Great Britain
by Amazon

38850979R00179